Secrets...
& Lies

...*Plus!*

DO YOU YEARN FOR FREEDOM?
TRY OUR FAB QUIZ AT
THE BACK OF THE BOOK

SOME SECRETS ARE JUST TOO GOOD TO KEEP TO YOURSELF!

Sugar
SECRETS...

...& Lies

Mel Sparke

TED SMART

This edition produced for The Book People Ltd, Hall Wood Avenue,
Haydock, St Helens, WA11 9UL

Published in Great Britain by Collins in 1999
Collins is an imprint of HarperCollins*Publishers* Ltd
77-85 Fulham Palace Road, Hammersmith, London, W6 8JB

The HarperCollins website address is
www.fireandwater.com

9 8 7 6 5 4 3 2 1

ISBN 0 583 34708 8

Printed and bound in Great Britain by
Caledonian International Book Manufacturing Ltd, Glasgow

With thanks to Karen McCombie

CHAPTER 1

● ●

OUCH!

"My God, Kerry, what's wrong?"

Sonja Harvey stared at her best friend, who stood visibly shaking in the doorway, her face puffy and tear-stained, her nose dripping pathetically.

"Oh, Sonja!" Kerry whimpered, her pink-rimmed eyes brimming with fresh tears.

"What's happened?!" asked Sonja, peering over her friend's shoulder into the Bellamys' house, expecting to see some sign of family tragedy. But all she could hear was the *EastEnders* theme tune blasting out of the telly as the Sunday omnibus started up.

"Lenses," gulped Kerry, pulling a ragged trail of loo roll from the pocket of her jeans.

"What?" said Sonja, frantically trying to

understand what was upsetting her friend so much.

Kerry blew her nose loudly on the tissue.

"*Lenses* – I just put my new contact lenses in!"

"That's it?" Sonja put her hands on her hips and stared despairingly at Kerry. "You completely freak me out over a couple of bits of plastic?"

"Well, *you* try sticking them in your eyes and see how you like it!"

Kerry wasn't in the mood for any more hassle. Her mum and dad were already losing patience with her. They hadn't forked out a hundred pounds after months of nagging and pleading only to hear Kerry whingeing about the pain as soon as she put the lenses anywhere near her eyes.

It hadn't helped that her little brother Lewis had insisted on sitting on the edge of the bath to watch, laughing at her attempts to get them in. Then, to cap it all, she'd found that Barney – in lieu of pudding after his morning's Winalot – had eaten the instruction leaflet that came with the lens cleaning fluid. The excruciating nipping in her eyes had got worse, not better, since she'd finally put them in (at attempt number eleven), and now Sonja was about to start...

"Kerry, I just don't know why you bothered getting those things—"

Sonja was going to rant on some more about how much Kerry's little wire-rimmed specs really suited her – how they made a feature of the sprinkling of freckles on her nose – when she spotted how downcast her friend looked.

Kerry wasn't the type to say, "It's all right for you...", but Sonja knew deep down that Kerry sometimes felt inadequate beside her. How she wished for Sonja's mane of shiny, honey-blonde hair instead of her own unruly frizz of curls. How she compared her own girly curves unfavourably with Sonja's sporty, lean body.

So Kerry wanted to ditch her specs. If it made her feel better about herself then why not? Sonja decided to shut up for once.

• • •

"Do you feel better being out in the fresh air?"

The two girls were on their way to the End-of-the-Line café.

"Yes," lied Kerry, determined to ride through the stinging pain and the weird sensation the lenses gave her of walking two feet above the ground. She squinted at the traffic zooming by and tried to get her perspective back.

"Anyway, I've got some great gossip for you – this'll take your mind off those stupid things. You know how I went along with Matt to that golf club do last night?"

Kerry nodded. Sonja was meant to have been helping her babysit Lewis but, after a desperate phone call from Matt, had ended up keeping him company instead.

DJing for a bunch of middle-aged golfers in pastel sweaters wasn't exactly Matt Ryan's normal style, but he'd done it as a favour to his father. Or, to be more exact, his father – who used the club and its members for a little light networking – had threatened to pull Matt's allowance that month if he didn't play ball. It just cracked Sonja up that Matt had asked her along and not Ollie or Joe – mainly because he didn't want to lose face in front of his mates.

"Well, it turns out Nick's got a new girlfriend!"

"So? Nick's *always* got a new girlfriend," said Kerry, blinking furiously. "Every time we hang out at the café, he's boasting about the latest one."

"Ah, but this time it's different," grinned Sonja knowingly. "He's been going out with this one for three whole weeks and we've heard *nothing* about it! Ollie only found out 'cause he was teasing Nick about how he must have lost his touch. Anyway, Nick absolutely flipped and said that that was where he was wrong, then just clammed up."

Kerry had to admit that *was* weird. Part of the fun of hanging out at the End-of-the-Line café was hoping that Ollie Stanton's uncle, Nick, would come out from the kitchen and tell them all some long-winded tale or other. These usually revolved around the old rock bands he used to roadie for (everyone featured in the *Guinness Book of Hit Singles*, and more, by the way he spoke), his burgeoning business empire (the café and the second-hand record shop next door), and his success with women.

The fact that he could keep his latest exploit secret was pretty suspicious. And if he wouldn't even tell Ollie what he was up to, well something most definitely was going on.

"And there's more! Apparently, Nick's only gone and joined a gym!"

"What?" gasped Kerry, visualising Nick's belly straining above his tight jeans and thick leather belt with the Rolling Stones logo buckle. A serious diet of egg and chips in the café, and pints of beer in the Railway Tavern with his sidekick Bryan was responsible for that. "Who says?"

"Ollie does," Sonja grinned back, relishing spreading this juicy bit of news. "When he went to open up at the End the other morning, he saw Nick just arriving back from somewhere and go rushing up to his flat with a sports bag. He asked

Bryan about it later and he said Nick's been going to that posh gym up at the tennis club every morning lately."

"What do you reckon? Is he trying to lose his love handles for his new girlfriend?" suggested Kerry.

"Nah – I reckon he's met someone there. And I bet it's someone who's not really his type and he's embarrassed being seen with her. You know him – he always likes to have some glamorous young thing on his arm," said Sonja scornfully. "I bet he's seeing some rich, bored housewife or something. Bet this one's some woman in a hideous floral number who thinks Elton John's really rockin'!"

They giggled at the idea of Ollie's uncle trying to hold on to his street cred. Although they all liked him, everyone who hung out at the End thought Nick's taste in music (and fashion) was stuck in a time warp, circa 1975. Even Matt, who picked Nick's brains on every aspect of the music business, would end up nodding off when Nick went on about ancient bands like Status Quo and Whitesnake, whoever they were. All the stuff he sold in the second-hand record shop, basically.

"But of course, you realise the saddest thing here," Sonja suddenly sighed. "Whatever's going on with Nick, he's doing a lot better in the romance stakes than any of us."

Kerry nodded. Sonja was right.

"I haven't fancied anyone for so long that I've forgotten what it feels like. And look at Matt! He thinks he's Mr Gorgeous, but he's not exactly fighting them off with a stick. And for all her flirting, Cat's not doing so hot either."

Kerry nodded again as Sonja counted off their crowd on her fingers.

"Maya – well, she's never had a proper boyfriend anyway, and Joe's love-life's a non-starter. Hey!" Sonja's blue eyes lit up and she turned to her friend with one of those I've-just-had-an-amazing-idea looks that always petrified Kerry.

It usually meant trouble.

"Maybe we should get Maya and Joe together! What about it? We could do some matchmaking at the fair this afternoon – bring two beautiful people together..."

"Like *sure*," said Kerry, realising with relief that Sonja was just in wind-up mode. The thought of Maya and Joe together as a couple was about as likely as Posh Spice falling for Chuckie Rugrat.

A sudden bout of nippy eyes forced Kerry to rummage about in her pocket for another bit of loo roll. She was all out.

"Wait here, I've just got to buy some tissues." Kerry dived into a newsagent's shop.

When she came out, Sonja was leaning against the wall, looking suspiciously thoughtful.

"I was only joking about Maya and Joe," she said, falling into step beside Kerry.

"I know," sniffed Kerry.

"The two people I think should get together are... well, you and Ollie."

Kerry stopped in her tracks and stared at her friend.

"*What??!!*"

"C'mon – you'd be perfect together," said Sonja, completely ignoring her friend's outrage. "And Ollie's all on his own since Elaine dumped him..."

"Son! *What* are you on about?"

Kerry was annoyed. Why did Sonja have to say such glib, silly, downright *thoughtless* things sometimes?

She knew full well what had gone on between Elaine and Ollie! They'd parted on good terms a couple of weeks before when Elaine had gone off on a round-the-world trek – and Ollie had decided *not* to go with her.

"I don't know why I didn't think of it sooner!" Sonja continued, ignoring her friend's less-than-ecstatic reaction. "You're both brilliant people – you'd make a really cute couple!"

"Stop it, Sonja! *You're* just being stupid!"

Kerry burst out. "And don't you dare start stirring this afternoon – I know what you're like!"

"But—"

"I mean it!" Kerry warned.

Sonja found herself shutting up for a second time. She hadn't expected Kerry to get so wound up. She'd obviously hit a raw nerve.

Kerry, for the first time that day, forgot about her stinging eyes.

How could Sonja tease her like this? And how could she suggest that she and Ollie could ever be more than just good mates?

She couldn't believe it of Sonja! She was as bad as some of those stupid girls from her sixth-form college who always went on about how boys and girls could never just be friends: that old love thing always got in the way.

Well, they were wrong – all of them. She and Ollie could talk about anything, and she could be her goofy, ordinary self and not feel shy in front of him, as she often did with people. Nope, there was only pure, unadulterated friendship going on between them – no attraction at all.

So yeah, he's cute-looking and everything, but that's never mattered to me, Kerry thought to herself. *I mean, it's not like I could ever imagine myself kissing him, is it?*

Is it?

Kerry's heart lurched suddenly and she felt a strange, tantalising shiver shoot up her back.

Oh my God... she nearly said out loud, as a sudden realisation hit her like a runaway truck.

CHAPTER 2

• •

SONJA'S A PAIN

"Ahhhhh...!"

"Where *are* they?" Maya Joshi's muffled voice came from somewhere above Kerry. It was the third time she'd said that in the last five minutes.

"Ahhhhh...!"

"Kerry, what are you *doing* down there!" There was irritation in Maya's voice, but Kerry knew it was more to do with all the others being late than with anything she was up to.

"Ahhhhh...!"

"Kerry?"

"Ahhhhh... *choo*!"

"You OK?" asked a voice closer to hand.

Kerry opened her eyes and tried to focus on

Sonja, who'd bent down beneath the booth table to look at her.

"Did you find it?"

"Uh-huh," said Kerry, holding up a fluff-covered contact lens. "Ahh... choo!"

"Dusty under there, is it?"

"Yes," sniffed Kerry, rifling around in her jeans pocket for a clean tissue with her free hand.

"Well, I can see you're having a great time," said Sonja sarcastically, before adding in a whisper, "but I think you should consider coming out now. I just saw Ollie crossing the road towards the café."

The dull *thunk*! of Kerry's head hitting the underside of the table sent two glass salt and pepper pots rattling across its Formica top.

Sonja put her hand under the table and helped extract a slightly dishevelled and squinting Kerry.

"I told you that you should have gone to the loo to take your contact lens out when it started bothering you, instead of fiddling about with it here," said Maya reproachfully. "You could end up with an eye infection if you don't clean that thing properly!"

"Yeah, yeah," muttered Kerry grumpily, clambering over the red vinyl padded banquette and out of the booth. Sometimes it was so blatantly obvious that Maya was the daughter of two doctors.

"And I told you there was nothing wrong with your glasses. You really suit them! In fact, let's ask Ollie what he thinks when he comes in!" grinned Sonja.

"And I told you to stop it!" Kerry hissed back at her friend, before bumbling blindly in the direction of the loo.

Kerry scrunched shut her madly watering, lens-free eye and focused with her good one. At least that way she could make her way along the corridor at the back of the café without bouncing off the walls.

Suddenly, Anna Michael's face came into view, peering out from behind the gurgling cappuccino machine.

"How's your head? I heard that crack from over here," the waitress smiled, her expression wavering somewhere between concern and — Kerry noted — amusement. "Do you want me to take a look at it? There's a first-aid kit in the kitchen..."

"No, I'm fine," insisted Kerry, with an edge of panic in her voice. The tinkling of the old-fashioned bell above the café door behind her meant that Ollie had probably just walked in. The last thing she wanted was for him to see her in this mess. Before today – before that stupid conversation with Sonja – Kerry wouldn't have cared what she looked like, but all of a sudden it seemed to matter.

Breathing a sigh of relief, Kerry bolted the loo door. Now wasn't the time to analyse her new, jumbled feelings for Ollie. She would just have to try and get a grip on her emotions, and wait till she was in the privacy of her own room to let this one sink in. Thank goodness Sonja hadn't seemed to notice the turmoil in Kerry's mind as they'd arrived at the café.

Not that it'll stop her going on about me and Ollie, Kerry admitted to herself.

Once her friend got an idea in her head, it was pretty difficult to get it back out. Kerry had already vowed to strangle Sonja later. Matchmaking when it was just the two of them was one thing, but if Sonja was going to do it in front of the others, Kerry knew she'd just curl up and die. Like those little digs just now. Maya was way too smart not to pick up on them, and she would've done if she hadn't been more interested in worrying about where the others were.

Shaking herself into action, Kerry examined herself in the full-length mirror on the back of the door to see what the damage was.

It wasn't good news. Her black cotton jersey

had faint, muddy pawprints all over it courtesy of her dog, Barney, who had run in from the garden and jumped up to say hello before she'd left the house.

If that wasn't enough, crawling about under the table had made her hair stick up, and the eyeball that had taken a sudden and ferocious dislike to her new contact lens a few minutes earlier was now horribly bloodshot, and had sent mascara-tinged tears smearing down her cheek. And to cap it all, staring at her reflection with one functioning and one bleary eye was making her feel strangely seasick.

Turning away from the mirror, Kerry stuck in the plug and let a rush of cold water fill the sink. She sighed again and wondered where to start in her efforts to look even partially human.

• • •

When Kerry finally emerged from the loo, Sonja was hassling Ollie for more gossip about Nick's love-life. She was using her best confidential whisper – which could be heard as far back as the toilet door.

"So he's not giving anything away? No clues? No nothing?"

"Nope. Not a sausage," she heard Ollie

answer. "And you don't have to whisper – Nick's not working today. It's Dorothy's shift."

"Pity. I was just in the mood for a bit of gossip and intrigue."

Oh, please let Sonja behave, thought Kerry, walking towards them. *Please let her keep her big mouth shut...*

"It's lovely of you to join us," chirped Sonja brightly, as Kerry slid into the seat beside her. "We were going to give you five more minutes before we organised a search party."

"Oh, very funny," said Kerry, nudging Sonja along the long banquette.

"Sorry – haven't you got enough room there? Do you want to sit on *that* side?"

Kerry ignored Sonja's pointed efforts to get her next to Ollie, who was sitting alone on the other side of the table. The combination of the afternoon sunshine streaming in through the big bay window and Kerry's slightly blurred vision (now she'd given up and taken the other contact lens out too) gave Ollie a soft-focus, golden halo around his messy crop of brown hair.

Kerry shook herself and remembered the power of speech.

"Hi Ollie!" she said as casually as she could. "Where did Maya go?"

"She's just gone to phone around and see

where everyone's got to," answered Ollie, turning Kerry's insides to mush with his wonky grin. "I don't know why she's so worked up about it – it's not like you can miss the start of a fair or anything."

"Well, you know what Maya's like. Being late is an arrestable offence to her." *See?* Kerry tried to persuade herself. *We're just being matey as usual. Just mates. Nothing else.* But she could feel Sonja's eyes boring into the side of her head.

"Ollie, what do you think – didn't Kerry suit her glasses?"

Oh no – she's off, thought Kerry.

"Ah, right... I knew something was different, but I just didn't realise what it was," answered Ollie, gazing long and hard at Kerry's face.

This scrutiny was too much – she felt the heat of a blush spread across her skin.

"So what's the deal – have you swapped to contacts?"

"Yes," answered Sonja, before Kerry could get a word in, "but there was nothing wrong with her in specs, was there?"

"Um, no..."

"I mean, she was still really pretty wearing her specs, wasn't she?"

Kerry felt powerless. Once Sonja was on a roll it was like trying to stop a bulldozer.

"Yes, of course she was, uh, pretty..." Ollie shuffled in his seat, his mind probably racing, thought Kerry, to work out where Sonja was going with this.

"Of course, that's not to say she's not pretty now, is it?"

Right, that was it! Kerry knew there wasn't anything particularly pretty about her just now. One bloodshot, stinging eye and a face flushed bright pink with embarrassment weren't exactly giving her cover girl looks. She had to say something – anything – to stop Sonja in mid-flow.

"I'm sorry me and Maya left you sitting all alone with Sonja, Ollie. She's been rambling on ever since she called for me. Has she been driving you crazy?"

"Absolutely," Ollie grinned. "In fact, I don't know how I can stand to spend a whole afternoon in her company."

Kerry grinned back – this felt comfy again, just the way it normally was. Having a laugh, taking turns to tease each other. Just like mates do.

"Hey, you two could go on ahead to the fair on your own, if you want," said Sonja, all innocence. "Maya and me can wait for the others!"

"We don't have to wait," interrupted Maya, stuffing her phone card back into its correct slot

24

in her wallet. "I just spoke to Matt on his mobile – he's driving round to Joe's. They're going to meet us at the park, and Cat's just crossing the road now – see?"

"God, I didn't realise that Cat was definitely coming," grumbled Sonja. "She was moaning about it being just for kids when we suggested it before."

"Oh, give it a rest," said Maya, ever ready to keep the peace. "It's a beautiful day, so let's just all go and have a laugh, OK?"

"She's probably scared she'll break a nail on the dodgems or get candyfloss in her new hair-do..." Sonja muttered darkly, as her cousin hurried into the café, dramatically pushing her formerly blonde, now deeply mulberry-coloured, hair back from her face and breathlessly launching into a speech.

"Am I late? I didn't realise the time. I practically had to run all the way—"

"What – did your nail varnish take for ever to dry?" growled Sonja.

Cat stuck her tongue out at Sonja, while the others groaned. Sometimes the running banter between Cat and Sonja was boringly predictable.

"Just shut up and pay the nice lady, Sonja," said Ollie, nodding over to Anna who was coming out of the kitchen, precariously balancing four plates piled high with greasy fry-ups. "And get a move on. We've got that bet on about who can win the tackiest soft toy, remember!"

As Kerry stood up to go, she tripped over Maya's rucksack on the floor. Steadying herself on the table, she sent the salt and pepper pots spinning again.

"Kerry can't see a thing since she's taken her lenses out. She might need to hold on to you going along the road, Ollie."

Ollie laughed, then leant over to grab his jacket – giving Kerry the opportunity to shoot a look at Sonja.

"Stop it!" she mouthed silently at her friend.

Sonja just gave her a wicked Cheshire cat grin in reply.

"What's up with you two?" said Cat, immediately sensing something that she wasn't in on.

"Nothing!" answered Sonja brightly. "Ollie's just going to have to be Kerry's guide dog for the afternoon, that's all."

Cat stared quizzically at Sonja, then swung her gaze round to Kerry, narrowing her eyes as she tried to figure out what was going on.

Uh-oh, thought Kerry.

She had the funniest feeling that Sonja's behaviour wasn't going to improve...

CHAPTER 3

• •

CAT'S RADAR REVS UP

"No!"

"Yes!"

"I'm not doing it, Sonja!"

"Why not? It's a brilliant idea!"

Sonja's brilliant idea involved a cosy ride for two on the Ghost Train, featuring Kerry and Ollie, and presumably some fear-fuelled hugging.

"Look," Sonja continued undaunted, "it's simple! The three of us queue up – but at the last minute, I say I'm chickening out and that you two should just go on without me!"

"Sonja, for a start I do not want to be paired off with Ollie, right? And secondly, who would ever believe *you* being chicken about anything?"

"Jeez, you're no fun, Kerry!" said Sonja,

waving at Ollie who was walking towards them, carrying a cardboard tray of Cokes and hotdogs. "I knew I should have just gone ahead and done it without telling you."

"Without telling her what?" asked Ollie, sticking the makeshift tray down on the wooden bench, in between the two girls.

Kerry felt prickles of cold sweat on her back. What was Sonja going to say now? Why did she have to keep this up when she could see how close Ollie was? It was as if she *wanted* him to hear.

I'll kill her when I get her on her own, thought Kerry, the muscles in her neck knotting with tension. *That's if I don't die of embarrassment first...*

"I wanted to have a go on the stall where you shoot at ducks, but *she* doesn't approve," lied Sonja smoothly, nodding her head in Kerry's direction. "You know how she's got a thing about guns and cruelty to animals – even if they are only plastic. Isn't that right, Kerry?"

Kerry nodded numbly. Sonja wasn't one for lying, but when she did, it always worked, blending in seamlessly with the truth.

"Did I put enough mustard on that for you, Son?" asked Ollie, licking a trickle of tomato sauce from his hand, and crouching down in front of the girls. He was so close that if Kerry just stretched out her hand, she could flick that flop of fringe out of his eyes for him...

"No, but I'll forgive you," shrugged Sonja, pulling her long blonde hair away from her face and taking a bite of her hotdog. "So, how about the Ghost Train after this?"

"Sure, but shouldn't we wait for the others? They'll be back from the Big Dipper soon." Ollie rose up slightly on his haunches and looked over in the direction in which Joe, Maya, Matt and Catrina had gone five minutes before. But the milling crowds hid the entrance to the Big Dipper from view.

"Nah, the queue for that was miles long," said Sonja, through a mouthful of food. "Let's go – just the three of us!"

"OK. Are you up for it, Kerry?"

"Huh?"

Kerry had been so lost in thought – imagining her fingers running through Ollie's hair, feeling the softness of it brushing her cheek – that she felt momentarily exposed. As if Ollie could read her thoughts as easily as if they were displayed in a glass case. As if the words "I love you" were beaming from her eyes directly at him... This was too weird.

For a second, in blind panic, she forgot to

breathe. And in that same second, she felt the gulp of Coke she'd just swigged back hover – miraculously – half-way down her throat.

"Kerry! Are you OK?" asked Ollie, a microsecond before Kerry's silent splutterings exploded into a full-blown, Coke-spraying choke.

A dull thump caught her in the middle of her back, followed by vigorous rubbing.

"Is that better?" came Maya's voice from behind her.

"Uh-huh," Kerry muttered in reply, too breathless to answer properly, and too mortified to raise her head. What must Ollie make of her? Just this klutz of a mate of his, being even clumsier and goofier than usual.

Not potential girlfriend material, not in a million years, thought Kerry.

"I don't know! You didn't want to come on the Big Dipper 'cause you thought it looked too dangerous, but it seems a lot safer than choking to death on a stupid fizzy drink," drawled Cat.

Peering up through her watery eyes, Kerry – who was still bent over and being rubbed maternally on the back by Maya – could make out Cat's clompy, high-heeled shoes sinking gently in the soft, grassy earth. She felt like reaching over and pushing the sarky cow on to her fat backside.

Kerry often felt as though Cat was patronising

her, and most of the time she shrugged it off. But today, what with the hassle of her lenses, the shock of realising how she felt about Ollie, and now this stupid, idiotic choking fit, she had zero tolerance for any of Catrina's catty comments.

"You two are back quick. Where's Matt and Joe?" she heard Sonja ask.

"The queue was too long. Me and Catrina couldn't be bothered to wait. The boys are still there," Maya laughed, "mainly, we reckon, 'cause there're two very pretty French girls in the queue ahead of them."

"Yeah, it's a pity they missed your trick, though, Kerry. Y'know – spraying Coke out of your nose like that," added Cat. "Do you think you could do it again when they come back?"

Without answering, and without looking at anyone, Kerry rose to her feet, her damp jeans sticking to her legs.

"I'm just going to get cleaned up," she muttered, before heading off in the direction of the park toilets. She'd liked to have taken Cat with her and rammed her head down the nearest loo.

"Kerry!" Ollie's voice trailed after her.

Heart pounding, she turned around.

"Hurry back!" He grinned his lopsided grin at her. "You've got to hold my hand on the Ghost Train, remember!"

She may have looked a little soft focus round the edges, but Kerry instantly spotted Sonja – still sitting on the bench behind Ollie – give her a big thumbs-up sign.

And maybe her eyes were playing tricks, but she could have sworn that Cat was giving her a dirty look.

●　●　●

In the refuge of the deeply unpleasant, graffiti-decorated public loos, Kerry sat in the cubicle and sighed.

She could imagine the others now, all talking about her, wondering what had got into her. Kerry was always the smiler; the one who'd find something nice to say about everyone – the kindest of them all. They wouldn't know what to make of her coming over all huffy and storming off.

She'd only done that once or twice before; like when Sonja started hanging out with Ollie's twin sister, Natasha, and began neglecting her. She and Sonja had made it up, of course, but it had been a miserable, confusing time for Kerry.

She felt almost as miserable and confused now. Her heart was aching, and her pulse was racing so fast her head pounded. What exactly did she feel for Ollie? And if it was love, how could it ever work? Two people in a crowd going out together only caused hassle – look at when Catrina and Matt had tried it! That had been a disaster.

Then, without meaning to, Kerry shut her eyes tightly and tried again to imagine what it would be like to have Ollie pull her gently towards him and kiss her softly... but then opened them wide as a thought hit her. He'd never given the slightest hint that he liked her any more than as a mate, so what was the point?

What a mess, she sighed, and got up to leave. *It's just a stupid crush – I probably won't feel the same way tomorrow. He's my friend, and I don't want to spoil that.*

Then, just as she'd calmed herself down, a rush of excitement fluttered across her chest. What had Ollie meant about her holding his hand on the Ghost Train?

Get a grip, Kerry, she told herself. *He meant it as joke, right?*

Right, she sighed again.

Opening the door, she nearly walked straight into Cat and her not inconsiderable bosom.

"Kerry, you've been ages! Are you OK?" Cat asked, with what looked suspiciously like a fake expression of concern. "Ollie couldn't wait any

33

longer – he *begged* me to go with him on the Ghost Train. It was such a laugh!"

"That's nice," said Kerry drily. "Don't use the loo on the left – the flush doesn't work."

And with those words of wisdom, Kerry stepped past Cat, secure in the knowledge that Ollie really, truly, *sadly* didn't have a romantic thought in his head about her.

• • •

Kerry found Ollie and Sonja sitting alone on the bench, deep in discussion. A worrying sign, she decided.

"Hi, Kez!" said Sonja brightly. Too brightly. "I was just letting Ollie in on what we were discussing earlier this afternoon. Do you remember?"

Ah, thought Kerry, *so the torture isn't over yet...*

"Er, no," she answered, stalling. She didn't dare look in Ollie's direction.

"You *know* – about us all being disasters with romance."

"Mmm," Kerry murmured, sitting down on the grass in front of them, and hoping the earth might just do her a favour by opening right up and swallowing her right down.

"And Ollie said that just because none of us were going out with anyone, didn't mean no one was in love. Isn't that interesting!" said Sonja, in her best teasing tone. "Now, what's that all about, Ollie?"

Kerry glanced at Ollie and saw him wriggle in his seat, a grin playing at his lips. Did he look a little uncomfortable and shy? Or was he just playing up to Sonja – giving as good as she gave? Kerry couldn't tell.

"Like I say – who's to say none of us are in love with someone? It could happen." Ollie dragged his hand through his hair, unintentionally ruffling it till it stood up in peaks.

He definitely looks uncomfortable, thought Kerry, *and he definitely looks adorable...*

"Oh, come on – don't be shy with your Auntie," Sonja taunted him playfully. "Are you trying to say that you're in love with someone?"

"Well... "

The pause lasted an eternity.

"...yeah."

As Kerry stared at him, her tummy gave several giant-sized lurches worthy of a ride on the Big Dipper. Sonja, meanwhile, didn't bat an eyelid.

"Well, you can't stop there, babe," said Sonja, with an award-winning show of calm. "Who's the lucky girl, then?"

CHAPTER 4

● ●

OLLIE LOVES...?

"Hey – you really goofed there, mate!"

Ollie spun round as quickly as Kerry and Sonja, all three looking guilty, embarrassed and, in the girls' case, disappointed. A heartfelt confession had seemed to be a second away, but now Matt had marched right in to save his friend from revealing all.

Except he hadn't.

"Ollie, you should have been with me and Joe – wow, those girls in the queue for the Big Dipper weren't half coming on to us, eh, Joe?"

Joe Gladwin shuffled from side to side, and smiled awkwardly, raising his eyebrows at Matt's boast.

Right at that moment, Sonja realised that Matt

and Joe hadn't heard any of what Ollie had been saying, and that neither of the boys had registered the expressions on their faces. Matt was too busy showing off and Joe was too bemused at having had the attentions of two pretty girls directed at him. Via Matt, of course.

"They were probably staring at you 'cause they've never seen anyone wear so much hair gel," snarled Cat, strolling up to rejoin the others.

"Well, at least I don't dye my hair so many colours that my own mother doesn't recognise me half the time," Matt bit back.

"Well, at least *my* mo—"

"Hey!" Kerry interrupted. "Where's Maya? We'd better find her!"

"Yeah, where *is* Maya?" said Ollie with mock concern, swiftly taking up Kerry's lead.

Sonja gave a silent sigh of relief. Thank God for Kerry and her clumsy efforts at peacemaking. After a brief and deeply unsuccessful romance, Matt and Catrina were officially – for the sake of their friends – on 'good terms', but *un*officially ripped into each other at any given opportunity.

Matt and Catrina quit staring daggers at each other and started gazing around for the missing Maya. Thankfully, the tension that flared up so easily between them, Sonja noted, was just as fast to simmer down.

Most of the time their mutual tongue-lashing could be filed under just-taking-the-mick, but every now and then it went just that *little* bit too far – like now. Mothers were a pretty taboo subject for both of them. Cat's seemed to have had a maternal bypass around the time of her birth and these days acted more like a disinterested flatmate than a parent. And Matt's mum had created herself a whole new family, leaving her old one – which included Matt – *way* behind.

"She went off to that hoop-chucking stall," said Sonja, nodding in its direction. "She wanted to try and win one of those dinosaurs for Ravi."

"Come on, then – let's catch up with her," said Ollie, already on his feet and waving at his friends to follow him.

Like the Pied Piper, he led his little troupe through the ambling crowds, with Joe falling into step right behind, shuffling along, hands stuffed deep in his pockets. Catrina barged deliberately past Matt (and, without a thought, past Joe) ending up at the front with Ollie. Matt, striding tall and casually handsome as ever, was next, with Kerry and Sonja, arm in arm, in the rear.

Sonja gave Kerry a squeeze and shot her an encouraging smile. Kerry managed a watery one back.

Ah, thought Sonja. *That little bunny-in-the-headlights look again.*

It had been happening more and more recently, she'd noticed. That funny, startled but yearning expression that flitted across her friend's features when she forgot herself and just gave in to staring at Ollie.

Sonja had been making a real effort to be more attentive to Kerry since their bust-up over Natasha, and it was this new sense of awareness that made her suspect that there was some sort of a crush going on. But no matter how much she'd subtly hinted at it (and Sonja *could* be subtle when she wanted, whatever the others said), Kerry hadn't given anything away. But then it could be that Kerry hadn't even realised what was happening. Sometimes it took an outsider to spot the truth.

And Sonja had noticed something else – something that made her want to force the issue *just* a little bit. Unless she was very much mistaken, Ollie seemed to be showing signs of harbouring some more-than-just-friendship feelings for Kerry. That certain way his gaze softened when he looked at her; the way he smiled at her whenever she spoke... Could it be that two of her best buddies really were falling for each other?

Of course, she could be wrong, Sonja admitted to herself. But what was the problem with giving the pair of them a nudge, just to see what happened?

And she'd nearly done it this afternoon too. Her truly skilful piece of manoeuvring had got Ollie on the verge of confessing some secret – a confession that might have made Kerry blissfully happy, or at least put a lid on Sonja's theory.

Ah, well, Sonja reasoned, *there'll be other chances...*

• • •

Maya scuffed the rubberised playpark flooring with the toes of her trainers as she swayed back and forth on the swing. On her lap was the toy dinosaur she'd just won for her little brother. It had taken a lot of hoop-throwing and probably cost her more than if she'd just bought it in a shop, but she knew Ravi would love it.

"Look, if those French girls were as into you as you say they were, there's no way you'd be sitting here with us. You'd be off somewhere with them right now!"

Matt, perched on the top of the climbing frame, gazed down in the darkening twilight at

Maya and pulled a hurt face.

"What are you saying? That I'm making it up?"

Maya was always quick to pull Matt right back down to size. If it had been any of the others, he might have blustered out some smart comeback, but he never dared with Maya. She might be two years younger than him, but to Matt, sixteen-year-old Maya was as intimidating as any headmistress of forty plus.

"It's not that she thinks you're making it up, Matt," said Ollie, who was suspended upside-down on the climbing frame. "It's just that you have been going on about them for hours now. Of course, maybe what's bugging Maya is that she's not bored with hearing about them like the rest of us – maybe she's jealous! Ooouffff!"

A well-aimed, fluffy green dinosaur caught Ollie right in the stomach.

"We can take that as a no, then, Maya?" he gasped, clutching at the toy before it fell to the ground.

From across the lake, the lights of the fair twinkled in the hazy dusk, the last streams of colour from the setting sun giving way to the brightness of the ever-changing blue, green, red and yellow bulbs that flickered around the stalls and rides. A clash of music – traditional hurdy-gurdy organ overlapped by the latest dance tracks blasting from the waltzers – drifted over the water on the evening breeze to this quiet corner of the park.

Not that anywhere could be quiet for long with Catrina around.

"Ollie! Ollie! Come here and give me a push!" she screeched, standing on the swing next to Maya.

"Yes, Sir! On the double! One push coming right up!" said Ollie, untangling himself from the metal bars and getting his feet back on terra firma. Deftly he tossed the dinosaur to Joe, who caught it with the arm that wasn't busy pushing Sonja and Kerry on the merry-go-round.

"Make it a *big* push," Matt muttered to Ollie before he walked away. "You never know your luck, she might fall off."

For the sake of his other friend, Ollie tried not to laugh.

"I heard that!" yelped Cat.

"You were meant to," Matt growled.

"Oh, come on – you're not going to get all wound up by that grumpy sod, are you?" Ollie teased Cat. He grabbed hold of both the rusting chains and pulled her as far back as he could. Teetering in her stacked-heel shoes on the swing seat, Cat let out a giggly shriek of alarm.

"Not too high! Not too hiiii-ghhhhh!!" she

begged uselessly.

Dangling lazily beside them, Maya watched in amusement as Ollie put all his strength into shoving Cat high into the night sky.

Someone else was watching Ollie and Catrina fooling around, and it wasn't with amusement. Sonja, perched on the gently spinning merry-go-round, followed Kerry's forlorn gaze. Why was the sight of Ollie and Cat mucking about getting her down so much? It wasn't anything out of the ordinary – they did this sort of stuff all the time.

"Kerry...?" she heard Joe say softly, and turned to see him holding out the fluffy toy in her dejected friend's direction.

"Thanks, Joe," said Kerry, giving him a rueful smile. She took the dinosaur and curled her arms around it, resting her chin on its squashy head, looking for all the world like a little kid in need of some comfort.

Sonja glanced back at her friends cavorting on the swings. OK, so she'd had her suspicions today about how much Kerry really liked Ollie, but what was going on here? What was she missing?

In Sonja's analytical mind everything suddenly clicked into place. *Kerry* thought she'd sussed out who Ollie was secretly in love with. And she was quietly crumpling with misery because she suspected she was looking at that person right now.

Oh, Kerry, thought Sonja fondly, *you really are crazy about him. But you're even crazier if you think he's fallen for Cat. Especially after what went on between them before.*

CHAPTER 5

• •

KERRY COMES CLEAN

"Say it."

"No."

"Say it!"

"No!"

"You'll feel brilliant!"

"NO!"

"Repeat after me, 'I, Kerry Bellamy, do declare that I'm in love with...'"

"Sonja!"

"What?"

"What exactly are you trying to do to me?"

Sonja reached across the Formica table and grabbed her friend's hand.

"I'm trying to get you to stop lying about this – to me and to yourself. You fancy Ollie. So what?"

Kerry looked out of the big bay window of the café and blinked furiously, her heart pounding.

"Look," Sonja continued, "how many years have we been friends? How well do I know you? How well do I know you even when you try and hide stuff from me? I mean, I kind of had an idea that you liked Ollie, but after seeing how wound up you got last night... well, it just made me see I was right."

Kerry shuffled in her seat, but still couldn't bring herself to look into Sonja's searching eyes. She'd known this was coming.

When Matt had dropped her off the previous night, Sonja had grabbed her and hissed in her ear, "Tomorrow, after college, in the End – OK?" in a very definite manner. For once, Kerry had been glad of her parents' peculiar rule of not encouraging people to phone after ten at night, otherwise she'd have been in for an epic inquisition from Sonja.

"C'mon, Kez – why have you never told me? Me, your best mate?" Sonja needled some more.

"Because I didn't know myself till yesterday!" Kerry burst out.

"Really?" Sonja looked at her friend quizzically.

"Really!" Kerry replied adamantly.

"What, you're telling me that you've never, ever had the teensiest, *weensiest* ickle feelings for him?" Sonja grinned wickedly at Kerry.

"No!" she answered straight-faced, then shook her head and gave a wry, shy smile.

"Do I take that as a yes?" Sonja quizzed her.

"I guess – I guess if I think back... I s'pose I have sort of thought about him... *that* kind of way. Sometimes."

The expression on Kerry's face was somewhere between a grin and a grimace.

"Why did you never tell me?" asked Sonja, more gently, aware of her friend's discomfort. "We always talk about people we fancy!"

"Why?" said Kerry, shrugging her shoulders. "Well, what about he's my friend – *our* friend – so how could I ever think of him as anything else? And what about the fact that even though he likes me as a mate, Ollie would never *fancy* me?"

"What do you mean?" said Sonja, completely lost. Kerry sat across from her with her scatty head of curls escaping from two daisy hairgrips, her smattering of freckles, and her big, brown eyes fringed with thick lashes behind the glass of her specs. She looked as scruffily and messily adorable as ever. Sonja couldn't figure out what she meant.

Kerry clocked her blank expression. Of course it was hard for Sonja to grasp. When you were one of the most effortlessly gorgeous girls around, with bucket loads of confidence to match, it wasn't easy to understand what it felt like to be one of the legions of Ordinary People.

"Well, look at Ollie!" she blurted, her words tumbling out now that Sonja had forced her to spill. "Isn't he one of the most brilliant, funny, original..." Kerry waved her hands around in frustration trying to come up with more adjectives to describe him.

"Cute?" suggested Sonja, trying to help.

"Cute!" said Kerry in exasperation. "He's ridiculously cute too! How can I live up to that?"

"Live up to what?" asked Sonja, now sensing Kerry's lack of self-worth, but refusing to let her wallow in it. "Ollie likes you the way you are!"

"As a *friend*, Son, just as a friend. I can't kid myself that he'd ever think of me as any more than that."

"Why not?" said Sonja, watching as Kerry dropped her head on to her arms on the tabletop. "You've got every—"

"I haven't got every chance with him, before you start," countered Kerry, raising her head sharply. "How can I compete with someone like Elaine?"

"But Elaine's long gone!" Sonja protested. "She'll be half-way up a mountain in Tibet looking for the ultimate truth or something by now."

"That's not the point, Son!" said Kerry, her face flushed with frustration. "She was this amazing character, and Ollie was really into her. Beside someone like her, I'm so... so *dull*."

"Of course you're not!"

"And of course you'd say that – you're my best friend! And before you say one more thing—" Kerry glanced over as she heard Anna coming out of the kitchen laden with plates and immediately dropped her voice "—you're not going to tell me that Ollie didn't mean Cat when he spoke about being in love last night!"

"I knew that's what you were thinking!"

"Well, it's true, isn't it?" Kerry stared at her friend beseechingly.

"No! Ollie doesn't fancy Cat! Not in a million years!"

"It looked like it last night..."

"Nah – that was just their normal behaviour," soothed Sonja, even though she didn't completely believe it herself. Cat definitely had been going over the top attention-wise with Ollie.

"What, the way Cat was flirting with him all night? The way she grabbed his arm when they were heading home together?"

"So what if Cat was flexing her flirting muscles over our Ollie? It's as automatic to her as breathing. It doesn't mean anything!" said Sonja, trying to placate her friend.

"But all that stuff you got him talking about!" said Kerry despairingly. "That stuff about being in love! It's too much of a coincidence that he started opening up about that and then Cat goes all gooey over him..."

"Kerry, think about it," said Sonja firmly. "That time the two of them did go out together – how long did that last?"

"Not long."

"Exactly – it lasted about five minutes and it was big, fat failure."

"But people can get back together..."

"Only if they fancy each other in the first place! Catrina only did it to make Matt jealous, and Ollie only did it 'cause he felt sorry for her. It wasn't ever the romance of the century, was it?"

"I guess not."

"Well, see? My darling cousin, for whatever reason, was doing what comes naturally and ladling on the charm – Ollie just happens to be the only one of the boys who'll indulge her. Can you imagine it if she tried all that flirty stuff with Matt? Huh?"

A little smile flickered on Kerry's face. Cat wouldn't dare – Matt would laugh in her face after everything they'd been through.

"And Joe – poor Joe! He's all right when she's

buddying up like a bossy big sister, but he'd run a mile if she turned her full beam on him!"

Kerry's smile broadened. Even though Cat seemed to be growing fond of Joe in a little brother kind of way (despite the fact that he was a few months older than her), Joe was still pretty much in awe of her. There was just too much of Cat for Joe to cope with sometimes – too much cackling laugh, too much lipstick, too much cleavage. You could see him visibly shrink when she was at her loudest. But then they probably all did.

"Well, I'm glad we've got that sorted out because Maya's just walking up to the door and we're going to keep schtum about this, aren't we?" said Sonja, giving her a quick wink before waving over her shoulder at their friend.

Kerry didn't want to seem rude, but she was too agitated to sit and chat about all the usual stuff that filled their after-college conversations in the café.

"Hi, Maya! Sorry, I've got to run," she said, yanking her unfastened rucksack up from the floor, then gathering up the pens and loose coins that fell out of it on to the table. "Got to, er, do something for my mum!"

"Is she all right?" asked Maya, sliding into the still-warm red banquette that Kerry had just vacated.

"Yeah, she's fine," said Sonja, crossing her fingers under the table.

• • •

Watched by Sonja and Maya through the slightly steamy café window, Kerry turned towards home. But mid-step she hesitated, for the briefest of seconds. Her normal route would take her right past the record shop, and she usually waved in at Ollie whenever he was working there instead of at the café. He'd be there right now.

But somehow Kerry just couldn't do it. She was feeling too emotionally raw after the past couple of days, especially after the conversation-cum-confession she'd just had with Sonja. All she wanted to do was go home and hibernate in her room.

Swivelling round, Kerry stepped instead towards the kerb, waiting for the traffic to clear, so she could cross the road and be swallowed up in the anonymous crowds of commuters that were spilling from the station.

"C'mon," she muttered to herself, as the relentless tea-time traffic refused to throw up any gaps.

"Oi!" shouted a familiar voice behind her.

She turned to see Ollie standing in the grubby

doorway of Nick's Slick Riffs and was instantly aware of that familiar, uncontrollable, pink flush of embarrassment mingled with excitement.

"Not speaking?"

In a glance, Kerry noticed he was wearing his most beat-up trainers, a truly terrible pair of old, saggy, grey tracksuit bottoms and a faded black T-shirt that looked, even from a distance, suspiciously as if it was inside out. And, as usual with whatever Ollie chose to wear, he looked cool as hell.

"Hi!" she smiled feebly, still rooted to her kerb-side spot.

"Come on, I need you!" he grinned, waving her over.

If *only*... Kerry thought as she walked over and followed him into the dingy shop.

Its musty smell got her every time and she wrinkled her nose. It wasn't as if it was some charity shop where the donated clothes held on to the scent of years-worth of dusty wardrobes and faded perfumes. Old records and CDs didn't smell, for goodness sake, so why did Slick Riffs?

"Still stinks, doesn't it?" said Ollie, catching sight of her expression. "I keep spraying air freshener, but it doesn't seem to make any difference."

"Something didn't die in here once, did it?"

Kerry joked. Having something else to concentrate on helped her tension slip away.

"Maybe it's Bryan! Maybe he didn't go on holiday after all..." Ollie exclaimed, his eyes wide with mock alarm. "Maybe Bryan was too popular with the clientele and Nick was getting jealous..."

Kerry giggled. Bryan, an old buddy of Nick's from roadying days who ran the record shop for him, was what most people would describe as being on the comatose side of alive. The most customers got out of him was the odd monosyllabic grunt.

"*So* jealous that he murdered Bryan, chucked his body in the basement and worked up this whole story about him taking a holiday."

Kerry leant back against one of the many rickety record racks stuffed with old vinyl LPs and smiled as Ollie spun his tale. This was typical of him – going off on some flight of fancy and taking everyone with him.

"Well, just supposing Bryan is actually alive and well and moping his way round Dublin like he's supposed to be doing, what could make this place smell like so bad?" she asked, dangling her rucksack from her hand and staring round the tiny, dingy shop with its paint-peeling, poster-covered walls.

"Damp – that's what it is. And of course my

uncle is too much of a cheapskate to waste money on sorting it out," said Ollie. "Anyhow, discussing the damp course isn't what I got you in here for."

"Isn't it?" Kerry grinned, her heart hammering again.

"Nope. You're here to make some coffee and keep me company while I sort out the till."

"Fair enough," nodded Kerry, glad of any excuse to be near him, she suddenly realised.

"Two seconds – I've got to turn that round," said Ollie, pointing to the handwritten Open/Closed sign hanging from the back of the shop door.

As he went to pass her in the narrow aisle, Kerry moved back against the rack to give him enough space to brush by her. Her dangling rucksack, however, didn't do the same.

Stumbling as his shins collided with the crammed bag, Ollie grabbed hold of Kerry to steady himself.

"Oh, I'm sorry!" said Kerry automatically in the split second it took Ollie to regain his balance.

As the words left her lips, she suddenly became aware of two things: the warmth of Ollie's hand where it rested on her waist, and the fact that his wonderful, sweet face was just a kiss away from hers...

CHAPTER 6

● ●

A CLOSE CALL

The rattle and thud of the shop door being
pushed open made them leap apart.

"Hey, Ollie! Kerry! What's up?" asked Nick,
swaggering casually up to the counter. "Done the
till yet, mate?"

"Er, no, I was just about to," said Ollie,
running his hands distractedly through his hair
and striding after his uncle.

"How's it been?" Nick asked, pinging open the
till and thumbing through the pile of notes in the
drawer.

"Not bad. The afternoon turned out pretty
good," Ollie answered, throwing a quick glance at
Kerry, who was still standing frozen to the record
rack.

"All right, Kerry?" Nick nodded over to her as

he began counting out pound coins. "Just saw your mates Sonja and, er, what's-'er-name in the café. Making a hot chocolate last for two hours, as usual. What are they trying to do – bankrupt me?"

Nick was always moaning about how long they all stayed in the café and how little they spent, but it was all hot air. He knew Ollie's mates meant regular custom, and he knew he had a captive audience when he wanted to reminisce about his 'wild' rock 'n' roll past.

"Uh-huh," Kerry managed to mutter. "Bye..."

And with a crash the door closed behind her.

• • •

Kerry stared at her bedroom ceiling without seeing it; without feeling how uncomfortable and hot she was lying on top of the bed with her puffa jacket still on.

What did it *mean*? she asked herself for the fiftieth time.

Everything... nothing... she answered herself just as many times.

Once again – minutely – she ran through those last moments before Nick barged in. Ollie silently facing her, inches away. The pressure of his hand on her skin through her shirt. His soft breath brushing her lips. He'd leant, imperceptibly, closer to her, as if, as if...

But *had* he leant closer? It had all happened so quickly! Maybe she was nudged off balance too? Maybe she'd just imagined him moving those few, delicious millimetres nearer...

God, what's wrong with me? she chastised herself. All that had happened was that Ollie nearly tripped. He managed to pull himself upright. He'd been trying to catch his breath when Nick walked in. That was it. Finito.

Oh, but what if...

A scrabble of claws at her bedroom door and a shout of "KERRYKERRYKERRY!" heralded the arrival of Barney and Lewis.

"What is it, Lewis?" she asked, irritated at this interruption to her confusion of thoughts.

"Mum says tea's ready!" said the six-year-old, staring down at her. Barney flopped his head on the bed and gave her hand a soggy lick.

"I'll be down in a minute," Kerry answered listlessly and closed her eyes.

Sonja was right. There had been times in the past when she'd had flickers – more than flickers – of feelings that weren't just friendship for Ollie. The rewind button in her memory whirred back to that first time she'd looked at him and known – just *known*.

It wasn't any dramatic bolt of lightning and it wasn't any grand setting, that's for sure. She'd been at the café with the others one day when, on her way to the loo, she heard a commotion coming from the kitchen. Intrigued, Kerry gently pushed at the Staff Only door to the kitchen and peeked in. There was Ollie gallantly spinning Dorothy, the part-time cook-cum-waitress, round on her sprightly OAP legs, singing his head off to some old Elvis tune on the radio, while Dorothy shrieked with giggles.

Right at that point Kerry realised that Ollie wasn't just funny and entertaining, he was also sweet and kind. Right there and then, in the lino-floored corridor to the toilets, she had fallen in love.

She sighed. This was madness.

It was crazy to go reading anything into what had just happened, or not happened, back at the record shop. There was no use indulging in false hope. But then – and her heart sank further as she allowed herself this particular thought – what if in that weird, fleeting moment of closeness they *had* actually kissed? To Kerry, it would have been a huge deal; to Ollie, surely only a spur-of-the-moment whim. It would have been wonderful but terrible – the kind of stupid mistake that could spoil a great friendship.

So there was nothing more to it. Whatever the blip back at the shop, Kerry vowed never to acknowledge it, never to let Ollie suspect how she felt. It would be better that way.

A snuffling sound suddenly brought her to her senses.

"Are you crying?" said Lewis, still standing at the side of her bed. Barney snuffled again and licked the salty tear – as well as half her face – away.

CHAPTER 7

• •

CLOSER STILL

"What's that?" asked Maya, looking over Joe's shoulder at the CD he was examining.

"Dunno."

Joe flipped the obscure drum 'n' bass collection back and forth in his hand, recognising none of the names on it.

"I thought you were meant to be a musician?" Maya teased him, no more familiar with the artists on Matt's latest purchase than Joe.

"I only muck about on the drums. I'm obviously not as hip as DJ Matty Matt over there," Joe answered dryly.

"He's probably never heard of any of them either – just read about them in one of his trendy magazines," Maya laughed. Matt did tend to know his stuff when it came to dance music, but he didn't half take himself seriously sometimes – often boring his friends rigid with the finer points of the DJing business.

"I'd stick this on now to see what it's like, but we'd probably just get a long, drawn-out explanation about who mixed what track," said Joe, staring enviously at Matt's impressive sound system.

"Here." Maya stretched over to her bag and rummaged about in it, finally pulling out her CD Walkman. She flipped open the lid and handed Joe the CD that had been in it. "Stick this on – it's a corny '80s hits album I got cheap in HMV the other day. Let's see if we can't contaminate Matt's precious hi-fi."

"Excellent! He'll hate it!"

Oblivious to Maya and Joe's scheming, Matt was lounging on a bean bag on the other side of his cavernous room, deep in conversation with Ollie.

"So they definitely aren't looking for a DJ, then?"

"I told you, Matt, it's a '60s theme night – not your kind of thing," Ollie shrugged from the comfort of the oversized sofa. "And, as I keep reminding you, it is a charity concert. As in, no money..."

"What? You're playing a gig for nothing?"

"Yes, just like everyone in every other band on the bill."

"Well, at least you're making contacts, I guess..." said Matt doubtfully. For him, there had to be a gain in everything he did. Anything else was just a waste of ambition and energy.

"I'm not doing it for that," Ollie tried to explain patiently. "My dad put me up for this. He was a big fan of the guys who are putting this ska band together, and 'cause a couple of them still drop into the bar when they're passing, he suggested me when they said they were short of a sax player."

"So, you're doing it for Daddy, then?"

"No!" said Ollie, trying not to lose his cool. "You know I love all that kind of music too – as well as what me and Joe do with The Loud."

"Hmm," nodded Matt. His record boxes for DJing may have been packed with a wide variety of sounds to suit a wide variety of audiences, but when it came to his own personal taste, any music that went back more than three years and didn't have a dance beat meant nothing to him.

"And don't forget," Ollie continued, "starving kids are going to benefit from this concert."

Matt nodded, but looked as if it still didn't make any sense to him. Ollie felt a rush of irritation. He was really excited and proud to be asked to do this show and Matt, with his transparent lack of enthusiasm, was only putting a damper on it.

"So you expect us to pay to come all the way through to the city and listen to this old-fashioned drivel, do you?" Sonja butted in, a cheeky grin on her face. She knew how passionate Ollie was about anything to do with Mod stuff, and truly liked all the tapes of scratchy old ska and Motown tracks that he'd made up for her in the past. But it was also fun teasing him.

"Well, if it isn't *too* much trouble," Ollie grinned back, taking no offence and actually glad for a distraction in the conversation. Matt was a great mate, but he was so single-minded – he could never seem to put himself in anyone else's shoes or appreciate their point of view.

"Ooh, I love an excuse for a night out in the city," sighed Cat, finally joining the conversation after being glued to the fashion pages of her magazine for the past twenty minutes. "I can't wait!"

Ollie felt another rush of irritation, then realised what was behind it. He hadn't seen Kerry for a while. Where had she got to?

"I'm pretty hungry," he said, turning his attention back to Matt. "Is it OK if I grab myself something from the kitchen?"

"Yeah, sure," shrugged Matt. "You want to grab me another beer while you're up there? There's none left down here."

Ollie nodded and stepped over Cat's fishnet-clad legs. It made him smile, the way she dressed up all the time, even though they were just spending a lazy Sunday evening slobbing out at Matt's.

"Need a hand?" she asked from her reclining position on the floor.

"Nah, it's OK," he replied as casually as he could. Ollie wanted company all right – just nobody's in the room.

Bounding up the stairs two at a time, he heard Matt's voice yelling from the basement behind him.

"What the hell is *that*?" as Wham!'s *Wake Me Up Before You Go-Go* blasted out from his state-of-the-art CD player.

● ● ●

Ollie pulled open the huge fridge-freezer and gazed blankly inside. He wasn't really hungry. He stood bathed in the soft, yellow light, wondering idly if it stayed on when the door closed or plunged all those posh M&S ready-made meals into darkness.

A waft of evening air brought him to life and Ollie turned in the direction it had come from. The door leading from the kitchen to the darkening conservatory was slightly ajar and, peering through, he could make out that the door to the manicured garden was wide open.

Treading silently in his old Converse sneakers, Ollie crossed the expensively stone-clad flooring of the low-lit kitchen and slipped through into the conservatory. Above him, stars were beginning to twinkle through the plate-glass roof, and in front of him, curled up on the back doorstep, was Kerry, staring out into the shadowy grounds of Matt's vast home.

"Hey, stranger," he said as softly as he could, so as not to startle her.

Kerry still jumped, spinning round to face him, her eyes wide with alarm.

"Can I join you?" Ollie asked.

"Yeah, yeah, of course," she managed to bluster, although Ollie was already making himself comfy beside her on the step.

"I missed you," he said jokily, feeling her give a little shiver. "Aren't you chilly sitting out here?"

"Not really," she answered, resuming her inspection of the lawn and shrubs through the dusk.

Ollie stared down at the scuffed toes of his

sneakers and wondered how to say what he wanted to say.

"Kerry, have you been avoiding me the last few days?"

"No!" she gasped, after an unconvincing second's silence. She'd be blushing by now. He couldn't see for sure in this light, but he knew she would be.

"Back at the shop..." he began. "I... well..."

As Ollie's words dried up, he turned to look at Kerry and saw that she'd dropped her gaze to the ground, her head bent forward and a fizz of curls obscuring her expression. Without thinking, he lifted his hand to her face and gently brushed back her hair. The faint light from the kitchen fell on her profile, illuminating the slightest tremor in her bottom lip.

"Kerry?" he whispered.

She turned to him, her eyes wide and questioning.

Fingers still entwined in a tangle of red-brown curls, he gently pulled her towards him and felt the tremble of her mouth on his own.

CHAPTER 8

• •

TWO'S COMPANY, ETC, ETC...

"Your eyes look funny – all glazed. Are those contacts bothering you again?" Sonja asked, squinting at her friend.

"No, no – I'm fine."

Kerry sat down on the sofa next to Sonja and tried to divert attention away from herself as quickly as possible before anyone noticed that she was about to explode, burst, *ignite* with happiness.

"Where's your dad tonight then, Matt?" she said, faking interest. "It's very quiet up there in the house."

"Amsterdam," he replied, rifling through a rack of CDs. "Or maybe he said Aberdeen..."

Still in her reclining position on the floor, Cat snorted.

"There's a bit of a difference between Amsterdam and Aberdeen! Didn't you do geography at that posh school of yours?"

"Well, whatever – he's doing some business deal somewhere," said Matt sharply. "Is Ollie still up there, Kez? He said he'd bring me back a beer ages ago."

"Yeah," said Kerry, hoping her voice didn't sound as much of a helium squeak to the others as it did to her right now. "I, uh, I just saw him in the kitchen just now. I was just out in the garden getting some air."

"Forget beer, forget gardens, get on with what you were saying, Son," interrupted Maya, who'd managed to snatch the bean bag from Matt when he'd gone to rescue his speakers from being mauled by an ancient Duran Duran track.

"Well, I need Ollie for this story really – oh, there you are at last." Sonja motioned to Ollie to hurry up as he came sheepishly into the room carrying cans of Coke, lager and bags of tortilla chips. "Ollie, tell them what you said on the way over – about Nick!"

Ollie looked uncharacteristically blank and paused for a moment as he handed out various cans to everyone.

"Oh, yeah!" he nodded, suddenly coming to. "Yeah, Nick told me today that I'd have to bank the record shop takings myself on Saturday, and when I asked why he wouldn't be in to pick them up as usual, he said he was going away for the day..."

"Big deal," interrupted Cat, then yelped as Sonja nudged her with the toe of her trainer in an effort to shut her up.

"Wait – this is good," shushed Sonja.

"*Then*," continued Ollie, handing Kerry a Coke and shooting her a meaningful glance, "when I asked him where he was going, he went all kind of bashful."

"*Bashful!*" exclaimed Maya. "That's the last word I'd ever think of to describe Nick. He's even more full of himself than Matt!"

"Oi!" said Matt, chucking an unopened bag of tortilla chips at her. "Who do you think you are, coming to my house with your rubbish taste in music, then insulting me?"

"Don't forget – I nicked your bean bag too," mumbled Maya, as she tore open the bag with her teeth. "*And* I'm going to eat all your tortilla chips."

"Will you let Ollie finish?" barked Sonja.

Ollie by this time had settled himself on the floor and leant back against the sofa, one elbow casually resting on Kerry's knee.

"Well, as I say, Nick went all bashful, and just

said that he was taking someone away for the day. I said, what – like your new girlfriend? And he started faffing about, then sort of coughed and said yeah. Then he scarpered."

"See?" said Sonja, as though Ollie had revealed some amazing truth.

"See what?" asked Joe, through a mouthful of crisps.

"I reckon it has to be someone he's well embarrassed about, or someone we know..." Sonja said theatrically, pausing for dramatic effect, "or Nick wouldn't be so secretive. You know how he is normally – he loves showing off about his girlfriends."

"Ah, but Sonja, maybe he's gone all shy 'cause this is the real thing – true love," reasoned Maya.

Cat snorted derisively again.

"That'll be the day," she said, her voice laden with sarcasm. But her mind wasn't completely on Nick's love-life. Out of the corner of her eye, she was watching Kerry and Ollie – the way he was leaning on her.

That wouldn't be out of the ordinary normally – they were all pretty tactile with each other – but there was something different going on here. Maybe it was the way that Kerry was holding herself so stiffly, so awkwardly, as if her nerves were on edge. Or maybe it was the way Ollie's fingers were curled possessively round Kerry's knee...

Cat paid even closer attention as she saw Ollie turn and look up into Kerry's face.

"How are you feeling?" Cat heard him ask her. Kerry's face seemed frozen in confusion.

"Do you still feel sick? I could walk you home now, if you want."

Ah, now what's this? thought Cat. *This is the first we've heard about Kerry being ill.*

"What's up?" Sonja asked, turning to her friend in concern.

"She felt sick earlier... when I went up to the kitchen I found her out in the garden getting some air. Isn't that right?"

Kerry stared at Ollie, then nodded. Lying wasn't something she was particularly good at and she felt she'd implicate herself less if she just agreed wordlessly, rather than open her mouth and try to join in the lie.

"Do you want to go home, Kez?" asked Sonja, who only lived a couple of streets away from her friend. "I could call us a taxi."

"Nah, it's all right," said Ollie, clambering to his feet and holding out a hand to help Kerry up from the comfort of the deep, squashy sofa cushions. "The fresh air'll probably be better for her, and anyway, I promised my folks I'd get back early and help tidy up at the pub. They're short-staffed tonight."

Cat flipped her gaze from Ollie and Kerry over to Sonja, who seemed to be half-smiling all of a sudden. This was like a re-run of the other day at the fair. Some weird little thing was going on between the three of them...

• • •

"I didn't know you could lie so well!" giggled Kerry, enjoying the warmth of Ollie's arm around her as they sauntered down the long, darkened lane that led to the main road from Matt's house.

"I only do white lies and I only do them for a good reason – like being alone with you," he replied, squeezing her closer.

Kerry's heart surged. So much for her great intentions of pretending not to care about Ollie. How could she resist him? She still wasn't sure what was going on, but she wasn't about to complain.

"Good old Sonja," he said, out of the blue. "I wouldn't have dared to make a move if it wasn't for her."

"How come?" Kerry practically squeaked, her stomach lurching at the notion of Sonja disloyally blurting out confidences to Ollie.

"All that hinting stuff she was doing at the fair last week," he explained. "She's as subtle as a brick, isn't she? The way she was trying to pair us up... and the way you were reacting. I sussed then that I had a chance with you – that I wasn't going to muck everything up, you know, with our friendship."

Kerry smiled to herself and immediately thought warm thoughts about Sonja.

"You smell gorgeous," said Ollie, nuzzling into her neck and feeling her curls tickle his face. "But you always smell gorgeous."

"It's coconut – my conditioner. It's the only thing that sorts my hair out. Kind of," Kerry mumbled, immediately aware of how silly her words sounded in the circumstances. She also felt a rush of excitement: *always* smelled nice? How long had he noticed?

"Ollie?" she began tentatively, not sure what to say next.

"Yeah?" he answered softly.

"What... I mean, why...?" she stumbled out.

"What – you mean why this?" he laughed gently.

"Uh-huh."

"Well, I guess because for ages I've wondered what it would be like to kiss you and wondered if I'd ever have the chance."

Kerry felt her heart hammering above the sound of the gravel crunching under their feet.

"And because I think you're the most lovely, warm, *real* person I know. Is that enough?"

Kerry was silent for a moment.

"No!" she suddenly laughed, making Ollie start too.

"OK," he said, trying to carry on through their giggles. "How about I knew I'd fallen for you that day we all had a picnic down by the river. Remember?"

Kerry remembered it well. She and Ollie had left the others and gone for a walk together along the towpath. She couldn't remember what they'd been talking about – only that they'd stumbled on poor old Joe, in a right state. It was obvious that Joe had been drinking – in the middle of the afternoon – and Ollie had tried to sort him out, while Kerry ran back and covered for Ollie.

Still, why had that been The Day for Ollie? Kerry wondered, before another thought struck her.

"But you were with Elaine that day!" Kerry was unable to keep the surprise out of her voice.

"I know," Ollie acknowledged. "I remember what she was saying too. All that stuff about travelling being the only way to appreciate nature and get to see real people. And there you were –

helping me, helping Joe. Doing stuff that mattered."

"What do you mean?" asked Kerry, desperate to understand every tiny detail.

"Well, I realised right then that Elaine was one of those people who's always searching for something, thinking brilliant things are far away in the distance. But you – you appreciate what's around you now. People, friends – everything."

"Do I?" said Kerry, not really sure she understood completely, but too thrilled to ask him to explain it any further.

"C'mere, you," Ollie laughed again, pulling her to him and wrapping his arms round her waist. Standing in the unlit lane, with the smell of wild honeysuckle wafting all around them, they kissed for the second time that night.

"Yoo-hoo!"

Ollie and Kerry sprang apart.

"Is that you guys? I can't see a thing!"

"Cat?" said Ollie, trying to focus on the figure that was clip-clopping in high heels towards them.

"Hi! I thought you two could do with some company!"

CHAPTER 9

•••••••••••••••••••••••••••••

NOT QUITE TEN

"On a scale of one to ten..."

"Nine and a half."

"Why? Why not a full-blown ten?"

Kerry swirled the spoon around in her cappuccino and shrugged. She still felt a little bit shy talking about Ollie, even though her voice was being practically drowned out in the café today. There were a whole load of little kids in, with accompanying mums, all stuffing their faces with sundaes and yelling their lungs out.

"I guess once I see how everyone reacts to me and Ollie being together, then I can relax. *Then* I can be ten-out-of-ten happy," she said finally, above the din.

"Well, everyone sounded pretty pleased for you when I told them."

Kerry looked up at her friend, curiosity burning in her eyes. Sonja had offered to spill the beans to the others to spare Kerry and Ollie having to make any awkward 'announcements' about their new status. Sonja had guessed what was going on when they'd left Matt's house together. The day after she'd popped into Slick Riffs after college and caught Kerry and Ollie in mid-smooch behind the counter.

"Is that a special offer this week, Ollie?" she'd joked as she walked in on them. "Every customer gets a free snog?"

"What did they all say?"

"Let's see," said Sonja. "Maya tried not to sound surprised – 'cause that's not her style – but I knew she was. She said, and I quote, 'Personality-wise, they complement each other very well.'"

Kerry and Sonja giggled – it was exactly the sort of thing the analytical Maya Joshi would say. It wasn't in her nature to be swept away by the spirit of romance.

"Matt just went, 'Whay-hey!' or some laddish thing, then started talking about himself again," Sonja continued, "and Joe said he was really chuffed for you both."

He hadn't really said that, but Sonja wasn't about to spoil the moment by telling Kerry that

Joe had actually been pretty weird when she'd called him.

"Hey Joey! Have I got some juicy news for you!" she'd blurted out.

"Uh, oh yeah?" he'd answered cautiously. But then Joe always sounded cautious on the phone.

"It seems that love is in the air..."

"Wha-what do you mean?" he'd stammered.

"Ollie and Kerry – they're together!"

There had been a long, long silence at the other end of the phone line.

"Joe – are you still there?"

"Uh, yeah," he'd said finally. "That's brilliant. Listen, I'm right in the middle of something. I'll, uh, catch up with you later, OK?"

Sonja supposed he was either gutted at the idea of having someone take his best mate away – although it hadn't bothered him when Ollie was going out with Elaine. Or he was annoyed that Ollie hadn't told him himself. But that couldn't be helped.

The kiddie racket was reaching epic proportions, while the mums fought a losing battle getting them to calm down. Kerry leant over the booth table to make herself heard.

"What about Cat? What did *she* say?" she asked Sonja, an unexpected quiver of unease disturbing her good mood.

"Cat? She was pretty intrigued, I think. Kept asking for more details." Sonja caught sight of the look of alarm on Kerry's face. "Which I didn't give, of course."

Relieved, Kerry nodded, but still felt strangely unsettled. Catrina was fascinated by the ins and outs of other people's love-lives – whether it was someone at school, characters in Aussie soaps or real-life film stars. Kerry certainly didn't want what she had with Ollie to be just another little entertaining diversion for Cat. But there was more to it than that... something else was bugging her.

"I thought Cat might have guessed about us already. I thought she might have spotted us kissing in the lane together the other night when she caught us up."

"Nah, I don't think so. She never let on anything like that when I told her," said Sonja dismissively. "What about getting out of here and nipping next door to see Ollie? The noise in this place is doing my head in."

Kerry nodded in agreement. Counting out some coins, she signalled to Anna that she'd leave what they owed in the saucer.

Scooping away empty, sticky dishes from full, sticky children, Anna gave her a wave of acknowledgement and mouthed the word "Help!"

She seems good fun, thought Kerry, as she and Sonja headed out into the much more relaxing sound of roaring traffic. Anna kept to herself most of the time, but these rare glimpses of her sense of humour always intrigued Kerry, and she made a mental note there and then to try to get to know her better.

"It's funny with Anna, isn't it?" said Kerry a little later, perched on a rickety old stool in the back room of Slick Riffs. "She's always so friendly, but I still feel like I hardly know her."

"Uh-huh," agreed Sonja distractedly, inspecting a moth-eaten chair before she dared put her bottom on it. "She seems pretty cool."

"Yeah, Anna is cool," agreed Ollie, coming through to join the girls having just got rid of a customer. "We always have a laugh when I work in the caff, but she doesn't give much away."

"Well, it's not as if you've got much time for chatting in there. You're too busy 'cause Nick's too mean to hire enough staff," said Sonja. "How you and Anna cope with just Dorothy and Irene helping out I'll never know."

"*Tell* me about it," Ollie sighed. He'd agreed to help his uncle out temporarily at the End when he left school last summer, but in the absence of anything better coming along, it had become a little more permanent than Ollie had planned.

Yet he did love the liveliness of the café and the banter he had with his 'girls', Dorothy and Irene, both of whom were well into their sixties and doted on Ollie. And he loved it when he got to help out in the record shop too, as he had this past couple of weeks.

"Of course, it would help if Nick actually worked a whole shift now and again, instead of sloping off to wholesalers and trade fairs and whatever else he makes excuses to do."

"Or whisking mystery girlfriends away for days out," said Sonja.

"Ah now, Sonja, I can't blame him for that," grinned Ollie, reaching over and circling his arms round Kerry's waist. "There's nothing wrong with a bit of romance..."

"Oh, yes there is," Sonja said with mock horror. "Like when my two mates go all mushy on me. Save it for later – *puh*-lease!"

• • •

Kerry heard the phone ringing and idly wondered who'd be calling at this time of night. She could also hear her mum trying to shush Barney – he always started barking along with the trill of the phone.

Two seconds later, there was a tap at her bedroom door.

"It's Catrina for you," said her mum, peeking round the door and looking crossly at her watch, which translated as, "Can you remind your friends *not* to phone when your brother's asleep?"

Kerry ran down the stairs and, stepping over Barney, grabbed the receiver from the hall table.

"Cat?" she said apprehensively.

It wasn't like Catrina to make social calls to Kerry. It was fine when they were out in the crowd together, but there'd never been any big one-to-one buddiness between them.

"Hi, Kerry!" Cat's voice buzzed brightly down the line. "I just wanted to phone and say how brilliant it is about you and Ollie getting together!"

"Oh... thanks," Kerry answered self-consciously.

"I'm sure you'll be *so* happy," Cat gushed.

We're not getting married, Kerry felt like saying, a little taken aback by Cat's over-enthusiasm.

"Ollie's *such* a sweetheart!"

"I know," muttered Kerry.

"He's a real one-off – one of the nicest boys I've ever met!"

"I know," Kerry repeated.

"I mean, you don't get many boys who understand a girl's feelings like Ollie does, do you?"

"I guess not."

Kerry assumed that Cat was referring to the way Ollie had been really cool and still remained her friend after that whole disastrous episode when they'd gone out together. Not many boys would be thrilled to know they'd only been used to make another boy jealous.

"Like the way he still keeps in touch with Elaine."

Keeps in touch with Elaine? What was Cat on about? Elaine had only been gone a couple of weeks. She'd promised to send him the occasional postcard on her travels, Kerry knew that much, but nothing had arrived yet, as far as she knew.

"I mean, that business about her telling him it's not too late to join her..."

A cold shadow passed over Kerry.

"Even now, for her to beg him to change his mind – it shows how special he must be to her... Of course, you two are together now, but it's still sweet, isn't it? Knowing that your boyfriend is so popular."

'Sweet' wasn't exactly the word Kerry would have chosen.

CHAPTER 10

● ●

FIRST DATE – LAST DATE?

Glancing round Burger King, Kerry could see no sign of Ollie.

Good, she thought. She'd been far too fidgety and uptight to fix herself up properly at home, so at least this gave her a chance to nip to the loo and see how bad/good/dishevelled she really looked.

The smell of cleaning fluid caught the back of her throat and made her eyes water. Kerry felt slightly alarmed. This was only the third time she'd braved her contact lenses in public and she hoped they weren't going to play up again.

Grabbing a piece of loo roll, she leaned towards the brightly lit mirror and dabbed her eyes gingerly. That done, and glad of the emptiness of the toilets, she stepped back and gave herself a critical once-over.

Hair: behaving badly as usual. The new, skinny, black hairband she'd bought didn't feel particularly stable and she suspected her rebellious curls might just spring it off her head at any minute.

Face: everything in place, but – God! – there was the start of a pink flush already, and she hadn't even met up with Ollie yet!

Clothes: OK white fitted T-shirt (she wished she'd worn her blue top – she was bound to spill something on this one) and smartish black trousers (she wished she'd worn her comfy combats).

Kerry sighed at her reflection. This was supposed to be a special night, but she didn't feel very special. This was her first proper date with Ollie. No hanging about in the café or record shop; no hanging around with the others. Just Kerry and Ollie. And the ghost of Elaine...

Stop it! Kerry told herself. Ever since she'd spoken to Catrina on the phone, she hadn't been able to shake off the thought of Elaine and of how much she might still mean to Ollie. Sonja, of course, had told her it was all nonsense.

"What's she on about?" Sonja had exclaimed when Kerry had phoned her immediately after Cat's call. "No way is he in touch with E! She's trekking round Outer-sodding Mongolia or wherever. How many phones or post offices do you think she comes across?"

"I know, I know," Kerry had mumbled unhappily.

"And," Sonja ranted on, "if Ollie was by some kind of miracle in contact with her, he'd have told us, wouldn't he? He wouldn't have kept that from us – he's got no reason to!"

Unless he's still slightly in love with her, worried Kerry, brushing dog hairs off her white T-shirt. Gathering up her jacket and bag, she left the sanctuary of the loos and headed back out into the loud, bustling burger bar.

Kerry sipped her coffee, thinking how different it tasted from the cappuccino spat out by the ancient, gurgling machine back at the End-of-the-Line café. She wondered if the others would be there now, chatting and laughing companionably in their favourite booth, while she sat here gazing out at the drizzly high street. On her own.

Burger King wasn't the main venue for their date, naturally; it was just a handy spot to meet up before they went on to The Bell, round the corner. It had been Ollie's idea to meet somewhere away from the others and to go out on their own.

They were going to check out a band at The Bell. Mick – who used to play guitar in Ollie and

Joe's band, The Loud – had got himself a new group. Kerry used to quite fancy Mick at the same time as Sonja used to fancy his mate Rob, who'd been in the band too.

It should be fun tonight, Kerry told herself. *If Ollie ever comes...*

Forty minutes and two cups of cold coffee later, Ollie came barging through the door.

"Kez! I'm so sorry!" he said breathlessly, flopping down into the plastic seat opposite her.

Kerry, who'd spent the best part of an hour fretting herself into a frazzled tangle of nerves, didn't know quite what she was meant to say.

"Uh, it's OK..." she muttered eventually. After having convinced herself that Ollie had either decided he'd made a terrible mistake *or* been run over by a bus (in her fragile state of mind, Kerry wasn't sure which option she preferred), she was too much on edge to say anything more.

"It was Cat," gasped Ollie, his breath not quite steadying. "She came into the shop just as I was closing up."

It still didn't add up. So Cat had dropped by – why did that make him so late?

"She was just wittering on about a load of old rubbish – you know what she's like," he said, sounding more like himself. "I just couldn't get rid of her!"

You couldn't have tried that hard, thought Kerry's frazzled, hurt, distrustful side.

"Are you OK?" he asked, reaching out for her hand.

"Uh-huh."

Kerry tried hard to stop her teeth from clenching *quite* so tightly.

● ● ●

The band was much better than Ollie had expected. The venue at the back of The Bell pub was mobbed, and Ollie and Kerry were so late that they had to stand at the back, peering over the heads of the massed punters.

Craning his neck, Ollie could see the lead singer – a girl with an amazing voice – dancing around the stage and singing over the top of Mick's thundering guitar. Although his main reaction was to be impressed, Ollie also had to admit to a twinge of jealousy. His own band – The Loud – had only played a couple of gigs, and was at a standstill since Mick and Rob had decided to leave. And now here was Mick with his new band – sounding brilliant.

Right there and then, Ollie made a promise to himself that once this charity gig was out of the way, he would concentrate on his own music. He needed to have a long chat with Joe about getting the band up and running again – they should discuss where to advertise for new musicians.

The twinge of jealousy he'd felt suddenly evaporated and, full of new-found enthusiasm, Ollie turned to grin at Kerry.

He was shocked to see how miserable she looked. So caught up in getting to The Bell in time to catch the start of the band's set and his fascination at seeing how Mick was doing, Ollie hadn't really paid her that much attention.

But Kerry would understand that, wouldn't she? Not by the expression on her face...

"Are you OK?" he yelled in her ear.

Kerry nodded, but didn't meet his gaze. Then Ollie noticed that even though she was standing on tip-toe, she was struggling to see anything through the forest of big blokes in front of her. Maybe that was what was wrong?

He darted away from her for a second and grabbed an unused bar stool from a nearby table.

"Stand on this!"

Ollie shoved the stool in front of Kerry and motioned to her to get up.

"I couldn't!" exclaimed Kerry.

"Why not?" he yelled back.

"People would stare at me! I'd feel really stupid!"

"Don't be daft – we're right at the back! Who's going to see you?"

He meant it jokily, but Kerry obviously didn't take it that way. Straight-faced, she clambered up on the stool and silently watched the band for the rest of the gig.

Glancing up at her from time to time, Ollie was sure that her eyes were glistening, as if tears were just a moment away.

What was going on?

• • •

The evening that the two of them had looked forward to so much fizzled out like a damp firework. When the band finished playing, Ollie and Mick had greeted each other like long-lost brothers, while Kerry hovered on the sidelines.

Now, sitting in the back of Mick's car, a bloke called Pete and a guitar case separated Kerry from Ollie, who was still chattering away with Mick and Rachel – the singer from the band.

Sitting directly behind Rachel, Kerry had a close-up view of her shiny, black bobbed hair. She noticed the way it swung cutely as she turned to answer Ollie, grinning a red-lipsticked, eye-twinkling grin especially at him.

See? she thought. *This is the kind of girl he*

really gets on with – someone lively, someone vivacious, someone not like me...

She turned away and stared out the car window, recognising a street sign close to home and feeling relieved that this torturous evening was nearly over. For her at least. Maybe Ollie would go back to Mick's – or even Rachel's – and carry on having fun after they'd dropped her off.

Absently tracing the track of a raindrop on the window, Kerry recounted every point of misery in the evening. The fact that Ollie had preferred to listen to Cat speaking 'rubbish' than meet her on time. The way he was more interested in the band – and particularly the very attractive Rachel – than her (he'd spent the whole night either watching them or talking to them). That tone of irritation in his voice when she wouldn't stand on the stool. Oh, and not forgetting those ridiculous contact lenses!

The minute they'd gone into The Bell, the smoky atmosphere had kick-started the whole pain process off again. She'd felt like a complete fool, perched on that stool, struggling to keep her eyes from spilling out stinging, lens-induced tears, while vowing to flush the stupid things down the loo the minute she got home.

The car ground to a halt.

"This is it, isn't it, Kerry?" asked Mick.

"Er, yes. Thanks for the lift," she answered numbly, as she wrestled in vain to find the door handle. She was mortified when Rachel leant over and flicked it open for her.

"See you tomorrow, Kerry – come in the shop, yeah?" Ollie's voice drifted after her.

"Uh-huh," she muttered, bending and glancing back into the car, but not managing to make him out through the veil of tears that had become impossible to hold back.

She slammed the door a little harder than she meant to, then heard the car speed away.

Well, that was good going, she thought to herself as she tried to stop her hand shaking long enough to get her key in the lock. *A first date anda last date – all in one...*

CHAPTER 11

• •

SURPRISE, SURPRISE!

"'Scuse."

Kerry lifted her bag off the table so that Anna could wipe it clean.

"At least somebody's happy."

Her mood of gloom disturbed, Kerry followed Anna's gaze across the road towards the launderette. Mad Vera, who ran it, was up to her usual tricks, singing along to the radio she always had playing, and dancing her way around the machines. Today, she'd turned her mop upside-down and was using it as a microphone, terrorising a young student who was clutching his box of washing powder tightly.

Kerry and the others often whiled away their time at the window seat, idly watching her antics. Usually, Mad Vera made her laugh, but this particular Saturday morning Lily Savage, Eddie Izzard and Vic Reeves could all tap-dance past the café window and Kerry wouldn't be able to raise a smile.

"Bad day on the planet?" Anna asked, replacing the salt and pepper pots on the streaky, wet table.

"Something like that," Maya answered for Kerry, returning to the table with two cappuccinos and a couple of Danish pastries balanced on an old tin tray. "But it's nothing that can't be sorted, is it, Kez?"

"Good," smiled Anna. "Right, I'll leave you to it. I'm officially supposed to be off for an early lunchbreak and I can see the cavalry arriving now..."

Maya and Kerry glanced up at the same time as the bell on the door tinkled and Nick came barging in.

"Sorry I'm late, Anna," he said breathlessly, "I just stuck my head around the door at Central Sounds when I was passing and they had this beautiful reconditioned Fender Telecaster that I just *had* to try out."

"Uh-huh," said Anna, dryly, arching her eyebrows at him.

"It was the spitting image of one Keith Richards used to play back in..."

"Nick," Anna interrupted him, "I don't care

about what year some over-paid rock star played his guitar. I'm supposed to be taking an early lunch so you can slope off this afternoon, remember? And if I don't go now, I'm going to end up with no lunchbreak left."

"Yeah, right. Sorry. But Anna – can you just give me two minutes? I should nip next door and remind Ollie that he's got to cash up for me tonight."

"No," said Anna firmly, untying her white apron and pushing it into Nick's palms-up, pleading hands. "I want my lunchbreak *now* and you've mucked my shifts about far too many times in the last couple of weeks."

Maya grinned over the table at Kerry. "Anna's really got Nick toeing the line, hasn't she?" she whispered.

Kerry didn't respond. Hearing Ollie's name and knowing that he was only next door made her stomach back-flip. She pushed the Danish pastry away from her, her appetite suddenly shot.

"OK, let's get back to what we were talking about," said Maya soberly, turning her attention away from Nick and Anna back to Kerry's disastrous date. She'd become Kerry's confidante for the day, since Sonja had been roped into doing something with her sisters and wasn't available to lend a supportive shoulder to cry on.

Maya delicately tore a piece of pastry off her sticky bun and got ready to make her proclamation.

"Right, I've thought about what you've told me, and I understand what you're saying, but basically—" Kerry automatically shrank from whatever stern and sensible words were coming "—I think you've over-reacted to the whole situation and got everything out of proportion."

Kerry knew this was only what Sonja would have said, more or less, but it would have been wrapped up a lot more attractively in upbeat words and big hugs.

"Look at it this way," Maya continued, tucking her long sheen of brown-black hair behind her ears. "Ollie's not like Matt, bless 'im. He wouldn't muck you around and flirt with other girls, whether it was Elaine or this girl Rachel. He's just not made that way! And Cat, well, much as I'm fond of her, I wouldn't put it past her to stir things a bit, just for her own amusement."

"Cat would never... I mean, do you really think she'd do that?" asked Kerry, aghast. She was always slightly wary of Cat, but couldn't see her doing anything *that* underhand.

"Maybe," shrugged Maya. "But then maybe I'm being a bit harsh. All I'm saying is, don't place a whole lot of importance on anything she's got to say. I think half of everything she comes up with is straight out of that fertile imagination of hers."

Maya's words did start to make sense to Kerry. Cat was good for a laugh – sometimes – but she wasn't the most reliable person in the world.

"And one other thing – I'm sure a lot of what you're feeling is down to the fact that you're mad at yourself for not just coming out and asking Ollie about Elaine."

That was true, Kerry acknowledged. She should have been brave and brought up the subject of Elaine, clearing the air there and then. But the time had never been right and the tension inside her had just got worse and worse as the night went on.

Maya paused in her straight-talking as the café door tinkled open and Joe padded towards them.

"What's new?" he asked, sliding into the seat next to Maya and pinching a crumb of icing from her plate.

"Kerry thinks it's all over with Ollie," Maya answered bluntly.

"Maya!" Kerry gasped. "Tell the world, why don't you!"

"It's hardly the world – just Joe!"

Joe's reaction was pretty hard to read. To the uninitiated, it could look like plain old embarrassment, but his friends knew it was more complex than that. Behind the blushing, startled expression Joe often wore, plenty more was hidden – they just couldn't quite work out what, half the time. Even to Ollie, who'd known him for ever, shy Joe could be a bit of a mystery.

"Sorry, I didn't mean that how it sounded," Maya apologised. She knew she could be tactless sometimes – she never did see the point of mincing her words – but she didn't like to think she'd ever hurt Joe. It would be like kicking the Andrex puppy.

"I know," he said, with a smile that didn't quite mask that funny, unsettled look of his. "So, what's happened, Kerry?"

She felt slightly uncomfortable with the idea of talking to Joe about Ollie. What if Ollie had already told him about last night and *his* version of events? Joe was very trustworthy, she knew, but it still didn't seem right to moan to him about his best mate.

"I don't know, we just had a bit of a weird night last night for one reason or another," she said vaguely.

"But she's going to get it sorted, aren't you?" said Maya firmly.

For a second, just as she glanced past him at Maya, Kerry thought she saw a flicker of disappointment on Joe's face. But, as Maya had so readily pointed out earlier, she couldn't really trust her judgement on anything right now.

"But how can I?" she whimpered. "If Ollie—"

"Kerry – this isn't just about you, or even you and Ollie." Maya suddenly seemed as grown-up and professional as her dad. Dr Joshi always made Kerry feel like an awe-struck five-year-old whenever she met him – either in his surgery or at their house. Now Maya was giving off that same imposing aura.

"It's about *all* of us. If you two have problems, it could affect every one of us and our friendship."

Kerry remembered the vow she'd made to herself not so long ago about not getting involved with Ollie for that very reason, and felt slightly ashamed. Of course Maya was right.

"I should go and see him, shouldn't I?"

"Yes," said Maya, nodding. "And right now."

"But I..."

"Nick!" Maya shouted unexpectedly, looking over to the counter behind which he was standing, the white apron now tied round his ample waist.

Kerry was confused – what was Maya playing at?

"Yep?" Nick answered distractedly.

"Kerry's nipping next door. Should she remind Ollie about cashing up for you?"

"Yeah! Nice one, Kerry!" said Nick, giving her the thumbs-up.

Without another word, Kerry agitatedly picked up her bag and left.

"Why do people make their lives so difficult, Joe?" said Maya wearily, after the door had juddered closed behind Kerry.

"Don't ask me," said Joe, agonisingly aware that he was making his own life difficult by choosing to be in love with Kerry. Although he didn't really have any choice in the matter.

"I mean, look at Ollie and Kerry – they're perfect together," Maya continued, combing her fingers through her sheaves of long dark hair. "But they're managing to make each other miserable!"

"I know," nodded Joe. But he was only agreeing to the first part of what Maya had said. Kerry and Ollie were perfect together. More perfect than he and Kerry ever could be.

They were his two favourite people and, without knowing it, they were breaking his heart. And there was nothing he could do about it.

● ● ●

The butterflies in her stomach were making Kerry feel slightly queasy, and she was glad of the blast of cool air as she stepped out on to the pavement.

She didn't glance back at Maya and Joe sitting at the window table of the café. They would have made her feel even more self-conscious and she didn't quite trust herself not to turn tail and run as it was.

She knew that seeing Ollie and talking things through was the right – the only – thing to do, but it was going to be so hard. What sort of reaction would she get? Understanding? Bewilderment? Annoyance? Anger?

Kerry still wasn't sure to what degree she'd exaggerated the problems of the previous night. But what on earth had gone through Ollie's mind?

I'm so stupid, she scolded herself. *I finally get it together with Ollie, and I risk it all by getting worked up about nothing!*

The door of Slick Riffs was in front of her. Kerry took a deep breath and pushed... but it didn't budge. She pressed her fingers more firmly on the chipped blue paint of the door and tried again. Nothing.

Puzzled, Kerry bent down and peered between the notices taped to the glass into the gloomy interior of the shop. Squinting, she couldn't make anything out at first. Then, just as she was about to straighten up, a slight movement at the back of the shop caught her eye – and her heart lurched painfully.

Ollie was stroking Cat's vividly coloured hair with one hand while his other arm was wrapped affectionately around her. Kerry sprang from the glass as if an electric shock had passed through it at the exact second that Ollie lifted his gaze and stared directly at her.

CHAPTER 12

• •

OLLIE EXPLAINS

"KERRYKERRYKERRY!"

"Not now, Lewis."

Lewis stared at his sister, who was huddled on her bed, clutching a pillow close to her. Barney was curled up at her feet, his chin resting on her knees, his big brown eyes staring dolefully at her. Kerry's cheeks looked wet.

"Are you sad?"

"Yes, Lewis, I'm sad. Now, you want to leave me alone, please?"

"OK," he shrugged, pulling the door closed behind him.

Then he pushed it open again.

"*What?*" Kerry half barked, a sob sticking in her throat.

"I forgot," he said simply. "Ollie's at the door."

Kerry dropped her head on to the pillow she was clutching and groaned. She wasn't ready to see him.

She'd only been in the house ten minutes and hadn't yet caught her breath yet from running all the way home. But she couldn't ask Lewis to lie for her and say she wasn't in. Lewis couldn't even understand the concept of boys and girls voluntarily *kissing*, so the intricacies of breaking up were way beyond him.

• • •

Standing nervously on the doorstep, Ollie glanced up as he heard footsteps on the stairs. His heart melted when he saw Kerry. With her hair unleashed from its clips, and falling in tangled curls, she looked like some tragic, Pre-Raphaelite heroine. He was trying to picture the particular Rossetti painting she reminded him of when the poetic moment switched to something more like a cartoon.

In a flurry of thumping feet and paws, Lewis and Barney thundered past Kerry and descended on Ollie.

"OLLIEOLLIEOLLIE! Kerry's SAD!"

"Yeah, I know, Lew," said Ollie, looking up from the little boy to his big sister, who was lingering behind him in the hall.

"Can you make her laugh?"

Ollie looked pleadingly at Kerry.

"I'll try," he answered.

"You'd better come in," said Kerry flatly, turning and walking up towards her room again. Ollie closed the door behind him and, wiping the hand that was covered in dog slobber on his jeans, followed her upstairs.

"Tell her a joke! She likes them!" came Lewis's advice from below.

Kerry took up her position on the bed and stared wordlessly at Ollie. He wanted to run over and gather her up in his arms right then, but he was too scared she'd push him away or even thump him right at this moment.

"Kez – it was nothing. Well, it was something – but not like it looked!" Ollie started. Then wished he hadn't – that hadn't come out quite right.

He stood uncomfortably in the middle of her room and wondered frantically what to say or do next.

"Cat's having a really bad time at home – she came in to talk about it and, well, she got all upset and started crying."

Kerry still said nothing. She wasn't going to make this easy for him.

"What could I do? I just gave her a hug, that was all."

Kerry looked as if she was about to say something, then stopped.

Ollie took this as a positive sign – he didn't have anything else to go on – and sat down slowly and gingerly on the end of her bed.

"She really is having a bad time, Kez. Her mum's being a total bitch – it's completely freaking Cat out."

"Is... is that what you were talking about last night, when you were late meeting me?" asked Kerry tentatively.

"Yes!" Ollie exclaimed, relieved that Kerry was perhaps beginning to understand what had happened. "It was just that she made me promise last night not to tell anyone what was going on. I don't know why, but she said she wanted to keep it between the two of us for now."

"But why was the shop door locked?"

"Kerry, honest, I don't know," said Ollie, little grooves of consternation appearing on his forehead. "I didn't realise it was locked until I tried to run out after you. I guess that the latch must have just sprung when Cat came in, for some reason."

He panicked slightly when he saw the brimming tears finally spill from Kerry's eyes, but felt a wave of relief when she gave him a watery smile.

"Oh, Ollie!" she managed in a wobbly voice.

He gave her his biggest grin and stretched over to grab one of her hands.

"Does this mean we're kind of OK?" he asked.

Hiccuping slightly, Kerry smiled and nodded.

"Brilliant! Now, do you fancy going out for a walk so we can be on our own? I can't help thinking Lewis is going to come barging in any second now with a knock-knock joke."

She nodded and smiled again as he pulled her to her feet and gave her the hug she'd been longing for.

• • •

"...And Elaine sent the postcard to me at Slick Riffs. Cat must have seen it the first time she came by to offload her problems – I'd propped it up by the till after I read it. It was just a picture of some hippy beach in Thailand with 'See what you're missing' scrawled on the back."

"But why didn't you tell me about it?" Kerry asked Ollie.

"I just forgot," he shrugged, "'cause of everything that's been going on."

Kerry looked at him quizzically.

"You and me, silly!" he grinned. "E's postcard wasn't exactly high on my list of priorities compared to what was happening between us!"

Kerry cuddled closer to Ollie on the park bench and rested her head on his shoulder. She tried not to be put off by the faint, cloying smell of Cat's perfume that still clung to his T-shirt.

"Who's looking after the shop?" she asked, jerking her head upright as the thought struck her.

"Don't worry – Joe's taking care of it," Ollie replied, giving her a reassuring squeeze. "I bumped into him on the pavement outside the shop – he'd come tearing out of the café when he saw you rush off. When I told him what had happened, he said he'd mind the shop till I got things sorted with you."

"Did he? What a sweetheart," said Kerry, touched by Joe's concern. "But won't Nick mind?"

"Nick? Nah – he'll be too busy rushing off for his dirty night away to bother about the shop," Ollie shrugged. "Anyway, I'd already asked Joe to cover for me, to let me get away a bit earlier this afternoon. I need to rehearse for the gig tomorrow."

Ollie was aware of Kerry's gaze. Her beautiful eyes were still slightly red-rimmed from crying, but were now looking full of hope.

"We're all right, aren't we?" she said, almost shyly.

"Of course we are!" Ollie grinned at her. "But it still niggles me that Cat got it all wrong about that postcard!"

Kerry was still pretty niggled too, but she was too exhausted from the last few days and too happy to be back with Ollie to figure *that* one out.

"But Cat's so messed up just now, I suppose she just got muddled and didn't really think about what she was saying or how you might take it," reasoned Ollie, kissing Kerry lightly on the forehead. "But, whatever, it's not as if she did it deliberately."

"No," Kerry agreed. Although somewhere at the back of her mind, through her haze of happiness, a little voice said, "Oh yeah?"

• • •

Catrina paused before she dialled Kerry's number. She didn't call her often enough to know the number off by heart and had had to look it up in her Filofax.

"Hello?" Kerry answered breathlessly, trying to wriggle out of her jacket. It was covered in blades of grass, she noticed with a smile.

"Kerry – it's Catrina. Are you all right?" Cat

asked, at first mistaking Kerry's breathlessness for some indication of her being upset.

"Yeah, yeah – I've just got back from the park," Kerry answered warily, wondering what was coming next.

She'd been blissfully happy when she'd left Ollie five minutes before – he'd had to tear back to the shop to do the cashing up before rushing off to rehearsals – but now a sixth sense told her trouble was ahead.

"Kerry, we need to talk. Can you meet me tomorrow morning?"

"But Cat, it's Ollie's gig tomorrow," said Kerry, flustered. What was this all about? Was it something to do with what she'd seen in the shop? But Ollie had explained everything...

"I know, but if we meet at eleven, we'll have plenty of time."

"Couldn't we do it another time, Cat?"

"No – it's really important. Look, I'll see you at eleven down at the End."

"Uh, OK, but—"

"See you then – I can't talk now. I've got to go," said Cat cryptically. "Bye."

Kerry stared at the silent receiver and shuddered.

Cat pressed the End Call button on her mobile and smiled.

CHAPTER 13

• •

THE LATE CATRINA OSGOOD

If Cat had sounded mysterious on the phone the previous night, she sounded even more so the next morning when she called to say she couldn't make eleven o'clock in the café because of "something major with my mum".

"What do you mean?" asked Kerry, slightly frazzled after a sleepless night spent wondering what surprises Cat might spring. Sonja had tried to reassure her that it was bound to be something and nothing when Kerry had phoned her about it the previous evening, but that hadn't helped.

"I can't talk now," Cat hissed down the phone. "Mum's in the next room. Anyway, can we meet later? I really need to talk to you."

"Uh, sure. What time?" asked Kerry, aware that Matt was planning to leave for the city about one o'clock, taking all the girls with him. (Perfect – a great bit of posing for mighty Matt!)

The charity gig was part of an all-dayer at Marshall Hall, the biggest and newest venue in the city. Even though it was still only 10 am, Ollie (being a participant) and Joe (who wanted to watch all the bands setting up and doing sound checks) would already be there. Ollie's parents had arranged cover at the pub especially so that they could act as his chauffeurs for the day and indulge in their favourite music at the same time.

"Well, four o'clock would be good for me," said Cat casually. "At Burger King. The End'll be closed by then."

"*Four?* But Matt's supposed to be giving us a lift at one!"

"We can make our own way to the city – we'll still be there in plenty of time to see Ollie. Oh, *please*, Kerry!" said Cat, her voice suddenly whiny.

"But it'll be too much of a rush!" said Kerry. She could feel her stress levels rising. "Ollie's band's on at half seven!"

Cat had obviously worked it all out.

"It's OK – there's a train just after five and we'll get a cab at the other end, so we'll be fine."

"But Cat, I really think we should maybe meet up another day—"

"Kerry," Cat interrupted with a new, solemn tone to her voice, "it's important. It's about Ollie and me."

Kerry felt a knot tighten in her stomach.

"What do you mean?" she croaked, her throat constricted with fear.

"Can't talk now – I've got to go and deal with stuff," Cat said, dropping her voice to a whisper. "Meet you at four. OK?"

Kerry held the receiver to her ear for a few seconds, even though the call was finished.

• • •

From the Burger King window, Kerry watched Cat sashay across the Plaza concourse, playing up to the guys hanging out by the fountain with their take-away burgers and skateboards in tow.

"Sod Cat!" Sonja had exploded when Kerry rang her to tell her about the change in travel arrangements.

"But, Son, what can I do? If it's about her and Ollie, I've got to hear it – whatever it is she's got to say."

"Well, if you're determined to let her muck you around..." Sonja had said theatrically. She didn't want to come across so tetchy, but she was angry for Kerry. She had a gut feeling that her cousin was up to something and she was annoyed with Kerry for letting herself be manipulated so easily.

Kerry felt completely hemmed in. She had known Sonja would flip out about Cat rearranging everything, even though spending the afternoon having this cosy, one-to-one chat with Cat while the others went on ahead was the last thing Kerry wanted. But what choice did she have?

Kerry watched apprehensively as Cat pushed open the door and came hurrying over to her. God – what was this going to be about?

"Kerry! I'm so sorry!" she said, throwing her arms around her friend and planting a burgundy-coloured kiss on her cheek.

Her heart racing like a winner at the Grand Prix, Kerry didn't know what to say – or think.

"Me and Ollie!" squeaked Cat emotionally.

"What?" said Kerry, desperate to understand what exactly Cat meant to tell her.

"Him and me..." She trailed off, dabbing her nose and taking a seat opposite Kerry.

Kerry stared at her in desperation. She just wanted to be put out of her misery.

"He... I... I didn't mean to upset you, Kerry!" and with that she started to cry. Kerry couldn't say a word.

"Kez, Ollie was just comforting me when you saw us together, honest!"

"I know," said Kerry after a pause.

"It's true – honest. He was just helping me deal with some stuff about my mum," Cat sniffed, dabbing her eyes with a tissue.

"I know," Kerry repeated dumbly, wondering if she could start to relax now. Wondering if they could just wrap this up very quickly and catch an earlier train.

No such luck.

"My mum, Kez – I'm having a terrible time."

"Oh," said Kerry flatly. That was bad, but not as bad as if Cat had said she was madly in love with Ollie and him with her.

Then Kerry listened and started to feel guilty. Cat had almost always had a bad relationship with her mother – they all knew that – but apparently it was getting much worse.

Sylvia had had Cat when she was only eighteen and was left to bring her up single-handed after Cat's dad did a runner. Now she was thirty-four with a great – but belated – career, and being a mum was most certainly not her number one priority.

("Mind you, she did draw the short straw, didn't she? I mean, you have to feel sorry for her, having Cat as a daughter," Matt had once joked. At least Kerry hoped he was joking, as she felt kind of guilty about laughing.)

"You don't know what it's like, Kerry – she's making my life hell! She's just being so bitchy and spiteful to me all the time!"

Cat had said as much to Ollie.

She must know he's told me this already, Kerry thought. *Why is she explaining it all to me now?*

Feeling slightly confused, Kerry managed what she hoped was a sympathetic nod.

"You know, it's like she's jealous of me – of me being young and attractive, I mean!"

Kerry doubted that. OK, Cat could be described as attractive, in a full-on, make-up-caked way, but her mum – for all her faults – was pretty stunning.

"But your mum's so glamorous and sophisticated – why would she be jealous of you?" Kerry let slip, not realising how the words would sound until it was too late.

Cat half glowered at her and seemed stumped for a moment, then her expression changed. Her eyes blinked furiously and her bottom lip started to tremble slightly.

"There's more to it than that," she said, pulling another tissue out of her bag and dabbing frantically at her eyes.

"What?" asked Kerry, flummoxed by the sight of Catrina's sudden distress.

"That's why I couldn't meet you till now! I

knew she wouldn't let up till it was time for her appointment for her precious leg-wax or whatever at the gym."

"What?" said Kerry, completely lost.

"Well, uh, she's wanted to have it out about something with me."

"What?" Kerry found herself repeating.

"Oh, Kerry – she's jealous because I– I– I've been seeing someone... and I think she's got a thing for him too."

It wasn't what Kerry had been expecting. But then nothing so far in this conversation had been what she had expected.

"You've been *seeing* someone? Who?"

Kerry wasn't so much amazed at the idea of Cat having a boyfriend – it was just astounding that she'd managed to keep it a secret from them all. She loved flirting and she loved boasting about her successes – a bit like Nick.

"I can't talk about it, Kez – it's, it's a secret. Please don't tell the others and please don't ask me any more. I've said too much already..."

And with that, she turned and stared tearfully out the window.

Kerry wondered if Cat would notice her sneaking a look at her watch.

• • •

"God, what's going on now? This is ridiculous! Oh, Kerry, I'm so sorry about this, really I am!"

Two minutes outside the city's main station, the train ground, screeched and sighed to a halt on the bridge. The lights of the city centre blinked away tantalisingly in the distance over the river. It was 7.20 pm.

For the tenth time that day, Kerry said, "It's OK, Cat."

For the hundredth time in the last two and a bit hours, she felt like crying.

The catalogue of events had run like some farcical plot from a corny movie. After their little chat in Burger King, there'd been that tense ten minutes when Cat had 'popped' to the loo, coming back full of apologies after 'bumping into' someone she knew and getting talking.

They'd still have plenty of time to make the 5.10 train, she assured Kerry brightly, before gasping and remembering that of course, unlike the café which was right next to the station, Burger King was a good walk away.

They dived breathlessly into the station ticket office at 5.05 – Cat couldn't run particularly fast in her stack-heeled boots – only to be told that the 5.10 was cancelled due to engineering works. The next train to the city was at 6 pm, but would be subject to delays.

And delays there were. Every time the train began to pick up speed it seemed to slacken off just as quickly, creaking infuriatingly to a standstill for minutes at a time. And now this so-close-and-yet-so-far stop.

"I just can't believe our luck tonight, can you?" said Cat, her heavily mascara'd eyes wide with disbelief.

"Mmm," Kerry managed in reply, picturing Sonja and the others checking their watches and glancing round Marshall Hall for them.

And Ollie – Ollie would be about to go on stage, nervous and excited, and happy that she'd be there to see him play. Except she wouldn't, at this rate.

"Honestly, Kerry, we'll be fine," Cat reassured her, pulling out a mirror and reapplying her lipstick. "Bands *never* go on stage on time. We'll maybe miss the first number, that's all. Guaranteed."

• • •

"That's a fiver each, please," said the bloke on the door of Marshall Hall. From the wide stairwell to the right of them, the muffled sound of music drifted down.

"Have they been on long?" Kerry asked

desperately, nodding in the direction of the music.

"Yeah, a good while," replied the doorman.

Kerry couldn't bear to look at her watch to see how late they were. Taking the stairs two at a time, she was only slightly aware of the thundering of Cat's boots behind her.

Barging through the door into the darkened hall, Kerry looked past the throng of the crowds to the brightly lit stage. There were about twelve people playing, dressed in old-fashioned Mod suits – skinny-legged trousers, skinny-lapelled jackets and skinny black ties to match.

Mostly, they were middle-aged guys ("the real deal blokes!" as Ollie had enthused to her the previous day), but there were a couple of younger lads up there – one of them being Ollie. He was playing his heart out on sax, standing and swaying in a line with a couple of trumpet players.

Kerry stood on tiptoe, straining to see him better, when the track they were belting out suddenly ended in a big crescendo, to the sound of deafening clapping and cheering.

"Thank you and good night!" said someone into a microphone.

Ice ran in Kerry's veins. She'd completely missed Ollie's gig – the one he had been so proud to be a part of. It had been great too, she could tell from the reaction of the audience around her.

Disappointment prickled in every nerve ending. She knew she was a nudge away from weeping uncontrollably with frustration.

"Oh, Kerry," said Cat, putting her hand comfortingly on Kerry's back. "I'm *so* sorry!"

For a second, Kerry didn't know whether to laugh or cry. So, to the shock of everyone around her and herself, she did both.

CHAPTER 14

• •

OFF AGAIN, ON AGAIN

"Cat!"

"Ollie! Oh, Ollie! It's terrible, we missed the gig!" said Cat, spinning round at the sound of his voice through the still thronging crowd.

Ollie's face fell. He'd already bumped into the others briefly and found out that Kerry and Cat were coming to the concert on their own, and he'd been dying to find Kerry to ask her why they'd decided to do that.

But she and Cat had missed the whole gig? He couldn't believe it.

"What happened?" he asked, glancing round for his missing girlfriend.

"Oh, it's my fault! I got in a muddle with the train times and then we got stuck on the train for ever," said Cat, waving her hand vaguely. "It was awful! I got so stressed out, though Kerry was having a laugh about it."

"A laugh?" Ollie said incredulously.

"Oh, yes," Cat nodded. "When we realised we'd only caught the very end of your last song – well, she just cracked up."

Ollie stared at Cat aghast. Kerry found it funny that they'd not been here for something that was so important to him?

"Where is she now?"

"Kerry?" said Cat, arching her eyebrows innocently. "Um, I couldn't find her when I came out of the loo just now, but I think I spotted her over by the bar, chatting to a bunch of lads."

Ollie blinked furiously.

"So I thought I'd just leave her to it and come and find you and the others, Ollie."

Cat had never seen Ollie look so hurt.

• • •

"Where have you been? We've been looking for you!"

Maya was relieved to come across Kerry at long last, but was slightly perplexed at finding her standing vacantly by a sink in the Marshall Hall loos.

"I was just waiting for Catrina," Kerry smiled

124

weakly, pointing at the row of closed doors.

"What? But she's outside. I saw her talking to Ollie a minute ago!"

"Oh, I *thought* she was taking a long time..." said Kerry, staring at the pale grey doors as if some kind of explanation might pop out of them.

She racked her brains. The last thing Cat had said to her after they'd come in here was, "Wait for me! Don't go without me!" Wasn't it?

Maya looked at her friend quizzically.

"Have you been crying? Your eyes look red..."

"Uh, no," Kerry lied, feeling too stupid after her tearful outburst to admit it to someone as matter-of-fact as Maya. "It's these contacts playing me up again."

"Kerry, you've got your specs on."

Flipping round to the mirror, Kerry was mortified to see that Maya was right. And it wasn't just her eyes that gave her away – her nose was red and damp too. There was no point in hiding it.

"I got in a bit of a state..."

"Why?" said Maya, putting a protective arm around her.

"We got here pretty late."

"Oh, Kez, you wanted to see Ollie! How much of the gig did you miss?"

"Everything, except for the last ten seconds..."

"Ah."

"I couldn't help it – I just started blubbing. So Cat took me in here till I sorted myself out. Then we both needed the loo and I thought I was supposed to wait..."

Kerry trailed off, feeling too utterly exhausted from sheer disappointment and confusion to finish her sentence.

Fishing about in her bag, Maya pulled out an old-fashioned silver powder compact and began dabbing the sponge on Kerry's nose. Maya's warm-coloured powder wasn't exactly the right shade for Kerry's freckly white skin, but it did manage to dull down the ferocious redness of her nose.

"There, that's better," soothed Maya. "Now let's go and look for your boy!"

• • •

"Ollie! Wait!"

After a quick post-mortem of the gig with his parents, Ollie was about to return to the back-stage area and help pack away the gear with the other band members. At the sound of Kerry's voice he turned, but didn't let go of his grip on the Artists Only door handle.

"Ollie! I'm sorry! We got here too late!"

"Yeah, Cat explained," he answered Kerry dryly. "She said it was all her fault for getting the train times wrong."

Kerry's heart, which had been pounding like mad as she tried to catch her breath, suddenly missed a beat. Something was wrong – *really* wrong. She'd never seen Ollie's normally animated, friendly face so stony and cold.

"Ollie? I– I'm really gutted about missing you..."

"Uh-huh? I heard you were having quite a laugh about it, actually."

Her mind racing crazily, Kerry tried to figure out what he was getting at.

Then it dawned on her. Had Cat told him about that moment, that split second, when Kerry had started giggling madly at the ridiculousness of the whole night? That split second before she started crying? Had Cat *mentioned* the crying part to Ollie? It didn't seem like it...

"But Ollie, I—"

"So who was it you got talking to all this time?"

"What do you mean?"

By this point, Kerry was completely stressed out. Her nerves had been so stretched for the last few days that she didn't have much energy left to figure out what the hell it was that Ollie meant now.

"Cat said she lost you, but then she thought she saw you by the bar with some lads."

"*What?*"

As soon as the words left his mouth, Ollie knew he was being stupid. The crushed look on Kerry's face said everything and, instantly, he dropped the cold front.

"Kerry..." he said, letting go of the door and reaching out for her hands. She didn't move. She looked too frozen to the spot with misery to respond. "I was just so disappointed when I came off stage and you weren't there. I must have picked it up all wrong from Cat. I'm sorry..."

Kerry felt his arms wind around her and his lips tenderly kiss her forehead. She'd had a miserable evening, but this made it all worth while. Almost.

• • •

"I don't like it," hissed Sonja. "She's up to something!"

Kerry, wrapped up in her happiness with Ollie, wished she hadn't told Sonja and Maya the whole story.

"Look, it's all just misunderstandings. It's just

one of those nights," she tried to reason, her voice dropped low, although it was pointless whispering. The thundering of the late-night train didn't allow for much eavesdropping from neighbouring seats, and a swift glance along the corridor into the next compartment showed that Cat was still very much engaged in flirting with some boys from college.

The four girls had all had to resort to the train after Ollie's parents decided to go on to a party with some of their old friends from the ska band, and Matt had ended up driving Joe, Ollie and various bits of musical equipment home in his Golf.

"She knew that train was cancelled. She deliberately made you late."

"Son, that's mad!" Kerry protested. "How could she know? And what would be the point of making me miss the gig?"

"I haven't worked that out yet," muttered Sonja darkly. "But all that stuff she told Ollie – that was out of order."

"It was just a stupid mistake! She's already said sorry, me and Ollie are fine, so there's no harm done!"

"You're too gullible and too forgiving, Kerry Bellamy," said Sonja, shaking her blonde head from side to side.

"And *you* seem to think you're in an episode of the *X Files*! There's nothing bizarre going on here. Tell her, Maya!"

Kerry looked pleadingly at her super-sensible friend. Maya gave her pretty nose a twitch and considered her response.

"It's too much of a coincidence. I think Sonny's right."

"God, you're as bad as Agent Scully here!" Kerry sighed.

"And all that stuff about my Auntie Sylvia being jealous of her and some new bloke... What a load of rubbish!"

"How can you say that, Sonja! How can you know that for sure?" Kerry kicked herself for spilling Cat's secrets. Whatever Cat was like, surely Sonja didn't think she'd make up something as heavy as that?

"Come on, Kerry – Sylvia? She's too up herself to care about – let alone fancy – some oik that Cat's supposed to be seeing."

"Oh, yeah? And how well do you really know your aunt?" asked Maya, ever the realist. "She hardly pays Cat any attention, so when did she last come round and let *you* know what's going through her mind?"

Sonja shrugged away Maya's common sense. It was ruining a perfectly good conspiracy theory.

"Well, I just think she's up to something."

Some frazzled nerve ending that had been stretched too far suddenly snapped inside Kerry.

"For God's sake, shut up!" she shouted way too loud at Sonja. It wasn't what she'd meant, but all Kerry wanted was for life to be calm and uncomplicated. For a change.

"Fine," snapped Sonja, grabbing her personal stereo from her bag and jamming the headphones over her ears.

Oh, God, thought Kerry. *Right now, the last thing I need is to fall out with my best friend...*

CHAPTER 15

• •

FRIENDSHIP FALL-OUT

Lewis and Ravi were perched on top of the climbing frame having a shouting competition.

Kerry and Maya were sitting on a park bench with their backs to them, hoping no one would suspect that they were related.

"It's been two days now and she still hasn't spoken to me," shrugged Kerry.

"Have you tried talking to her?"

"No..."

Maya sighed. Sometimes her friends seemed to make their lives so complicated: Cat in a tizz but still finding time to make mischief; Ollie going all huffy about nothing; Kerry letting herself get wound up; Sonja taking offence so easily... Thank God Joe and Matt were OK. For the moment.

"Look, I know you were feeling a bit

emotional, but you shouldn't have snapped at Sonja like that."

"I know..."

"It's not like you."

"I know..."

"You should tell her you're sorry."

"I know..."

Kerry's shoulders were sinking further and further down. Maya saw that she didn't have to push the point any more.

"So," she said, easing off the subject, "everything cool again with Ollie, then?"

"Oh, yeah," nodded Kerry, a smile automatically springing to her face. "Everything's sorted. It's really, really good."

"I'm glad," said Maya, relieved that her two friends had seen sense and worked things out.

"You know," Kerry sighed, "sometimes I can't believe we're really, you know, together..."

"It's hard for us to believe too. I don't mean that in a horrible way," Maya added quickly. "It's just that we've all had to stop thinking of you two as part of the gang and get it into our heads that you're, well, going out."

"You're OK about it, aren't you?" asked Kerry tentatively.

"Yes, of course! As long as you're both happy, and as long as it doesn't affect us all as friends."

It was something Maya was keen to get across. As far as she could see, it already *was* having an effect – that was the trouble. And if it got any worse, they'd all end up siding with different people and it would be all over for the crowd.

OK, so it wasn't a perfect friendship all the time. Sonja's bossiness, Matt's selfishness and Cat's, well, *obnoxiousness* could cause friction and the odd flare-up, but they all had good fun and were pretty good friends in spite of that. And after growing up feeling like an outsider, Maya wasn't about to give up on this bunch of people who'd made her feel as if she fitted in for the first time in her life.

"I know what you're saying, Maya! That whole thing's the reason I thought nothing would ever happen with me and Ollie. Well, that and the fact that I never thought I had a chance with him," Kerry laughed ruefully. "But, honestly, me and Ollie are fine."

"Well, how come he was so quick to think badly of you on Sunday night?" Maya felt slightly rotten at bursting Kerry's bubble of romantic bliss, but she really did want to know why people who were meant to be in love could mess things up so easily.

Before she answered, Kerry glanced round to see what the little boys were up to – it had gone ominously quiet. They'd moved to the sandpit and were silently and seriously constructing something using an empty water bottle and a discarded, broken spade.

"He was just over-emotional, I guess," she finally replied. "It was a big night for him, you know? After being so proud and excited, he was just really gutted that I'd missed it and—"

"—and didn't seem to care," Maya finished for her.

"You don't *really* suppose Cat deliberately tried to make him think badly of me, do you?"

"I don't know, Kerry," shrugged Maya. "I mean I usually tend to give her the benefit of the doubt, but..."

"You don't think she's lying about all that stuff she told me, do you?"

"About arguing with her mum?"

Kerry nodded.

"I think *that's* probably true to some extent – but the secret love thing sounds a bit far-fetched. It sounds like one of her 'Look at me! Look at me!' attention-seeking ploys."

"Really? You think she'd go as far as lying?"

Kerry should have 'gullible' written all over her forehead, thought Maya. All the others tended to be able to spot when Cat crossed the line between truth and fiction for dramatic effect. But

Kerry always tried to see the best in people – that was her problem.

"Like Sonja said to me this morning—"

"What, you spoke to Sonja this morning?" Kerry interrupted.

"Yeah, I bumped into her on the way to school."

"What else was she saying?"

Maya winced. She didn't want to get into being a go-between for them. It had been bad enough when the two of them had fallen out over Ollie's sister. Maya didn't want it to get to that stage between her two mates again.

"Why don't you ask her yourself? It's silly, you two not talking."

"I know, I know. I'll fix it! But what else did she say?"

"Well," said Maya, giving in, "Sonja thinks Cat's trying to break you and Ollie up."

"But that's mad! Why would she do that?"

"MAYAMAYAMAYA!" interrupted a voice at high volume. "Ravi says he's so hungry his tummy HURTS!"

"Oh, look at the time!" Maya gasped, checking her watch. "I'd better get back for tea. Let's get going, eh, Rav?"

"Yes, or Sunny will eat all of ours!"

Maya rolled her eyes at the mention of her

younger sister's name. She had forgotten that she'd promised her folks that she'd help Sunita out with her art project (which probably meant she'd end up doing it all, knowing Sunny and her lazy streak). All that *and* an essay of her own to write.

"I'll speak to you later, Kez," she waved to her friend, as Ravi grabbed her hand and started dragging her away.

"But—" said Kerry.

"Go home and phone Sonja," Maya called over her shoulder. "Get this sorted."

"OK..." Kerry answered dubiously.

What on earth was going on in Sonja's mind to come up with something like that? Things weren't quite adding up with Cat at the moment, but some bizarre notion of her trying to break up her mates' relationship *wasn't* the answer.

What a bitchy thing for Sonja to say! thought Kerry.

"KERRYKERRYKERRY!"

"What is it, hon?" she asked her brother in exasperation.

"Can we have our tea?"

"We already did, Lew – before we came out to the park. Remember?"

"Oh," said Lew thoughtfully, rubbing his tummy which had come out in sympathy hunger pangs with Ravi. "I forgot..."

• • •

"I don't like Ollie!"

"Huh? Since when?"

Kerry was taken aback by her little brother's reaction. The times she'd taken him along when she was meeting the others, he'd always made a beeline for Ollie.

Typically, all kids were drawn to Ollie. He'd have them giggling in minutes with all his goofing around and silly jokes. And all her friends liked Lewis – he was a cute (if loud) kid. She only lived in dread of Lewis opening his mouth one day in front of Cat and coming out with the nickname he had for her.

As a three-year-old, he'd said – after a visit from an over-made-up Cat – "who was that lady clown?" It had kind of stuck in Kerry's family ever since.

Uncharacteristically, Lewis stayed silent.

"C'mon, Lew – what made you say that?"

His pronouncement had come when Kerry had suggested they go and drop in on Ollie. The Swan, his mum and dad's pub, was just through the gates on the other side of the park. She felt like catching up with Ollie and seeing how he was enjoying working back at the End, now that Bryan had returned from his holiday and Ollie's stint at the record shop was over.

"Just don't like him," shrugged Lewis.

"Aw, you've got to tell me, Lew – that's not fair!" she cajoled him.

"He makes you sad," he said suddenly.

Momentarily stunned, Kerry stared down at her brother, who was trying to untangle a yo-yo from his fingers as he walked along.

"Why do you think that, Lew?"

"'Cause you see him all the time now, but you keep crying."

It was ridiculous but true, Kerry realised. Since going out with Ollie, she'd gone through times of being more upset than she could ever remember before. It was stupid! She was meant to be happy now that she was with the one person she cared for the most.

Right, she decided. *From now on in this relationship, no more misunderstandings, no more moping. Just bliss, bliss, bliss...*

"Don't be silly," she smiled at Lewis, squeezing his hand as they strode through the park gates and turned into the busy road. "He makes me very happy. He's like – like my *special* friend."

"Your BOYfriend, you mean," sniffed Lewis.

"Yep, my boyfriend," she laughed, seeing the slightly disgusted look on Lewis's face.

"Well, why's he snogging Catrina the Clown, then?" he said, pointing across the traffic-choked road towards The Swan.

Kerry stared at the vision of Ollie and Cat sitting together on a picnic bench outside the pub. Even from that distance it was plain to see that Cat's fingers were entwined in Ollie's hair.

And even at that distance it was plain to see that it wasn't the sort of kiss people-who-are-just-mates give each other.

CHAPTER 16

● ●

KERRY GETS MAD

"KERRYKERRYKERRY!"

"Shhh!"

"What are we DOING?"

"Hiding."

"WHY?"

"I don't know."

It was ridiculous to be standing behind this parked van, peering round the side to watch the movements of her supposed boyfriend and equally supposed mate. But right at that moment, Kerry couldn't think of anything better to do.

"You're not going to go all SAD again, are you?" asked Lewis, scrunching up his freckled nose at her.

"Nope," Kerry answered firmly. This time, she was going to get mad.

Glancing round for a clear path through the traffic, Kerry held on tightly to Lewis's hand and strode defiantly across the road. This couldn't be explained away just like that. *Let's see the look on their faces when I walk right up to them,* she thought. *Let's see what they've got to say for themselves then!*

Charged with righteous indignation and the need to keep her brother in one piece, Kerry was too busy in those few seconds to see Cat wobble up to her full height of 5 feet 10 inches (four of those inches comprising the heels of her strappy sandals), pull down her little stretchy skirt to a semi-decent, bottom-covering length, and take her leave of Ollie, after planting a full-lipped smacker on his cheek.

Instead of confronting two guilty parties as she stepped on to the safety of the pavement outside the pub, Kerry was faced with the sight of Ollie's back as he was about to step into the bar, clutching the empties from the table.

"Well, well! It looked like you two were having a good time there. A *very* good time," said Kerry archly, her anger giving her the confidence to do a Sonja and ladle on the sarcasm.

Ollie spun round with a look of confusion on his face.

"Kerry! Hi! What's up?" he said quizzically.

Although caught out by Cat's vanishing trick, Kerry was ready to reply with another sharp and pointed one-liner. She'd been practising them for the last five minutes while she and Lewis were impersonating Hetty Wainthrop behind the parked van.

"HAHAHA!"

A perplexed Ollie and irate Kerry both turned and looked at Lewis.

"You've got lipstick ALL over!" he giggled, pointing at Ollie's face.

It was true. Burnished Burgundy – Cat's trademark, lurid lipstick – was smudged liberally round his mouth and chin, while a more precise lip-shaped imprint decorated his cheek.

Kerry crossed her arms and waited silently to see how he was going to wriggle out of this one.

• • •

"Neeeeeeeeeeeeyowwwwwwwww!"

Lewis was in heaven, while Kerry, most definitely, was not.

Installed happily in front of the computer in Ollie's bedroom, Lewis was frantically manoeuvring the joystick and making stupid noises as he played the racing game Ollie had put on for him. That, coupled with the assorted bags of crinkle-cut crisps and Cheesy Moments (grabbed from behind the bar as pure bribe material), was just about as good as it got for this particular six-year-old.

Sitting silently and fuming furiously at the kitchen table, Kerry watched as Ollie emerged from the bathroom, scrubbing his newly washed face with a towel, and came along the corridor towards her.

"OK, so you saw me and Cat talking—"

"*Kissing*, you mean!" snapped Kerry.

"With tongues and everything! YUCK!" came a muffled voice, through a mouthful of crisps, from Ollie's room.

Ollie went over and closed the kitchen door for privacy.

"She was pouring out her heart to me again," Ollie began, pulling out a chair opposite Kerry. "She said it was a kiss to say thank you for listening."

"It looked a bit over-the-top for a thank you kiss to me," Kerry hissed, unconvinced.

"Kerry, when did you ever know Catrina *not* to be over-the-top – about *everything*?" said Ollie, looking at her pleadingly.

No, no, no, thought Kerry. *You're not getting away with it that easily*. She crossed her arms again and stared wordlessly out of the window at the cloudy skyline, doing her usual de-stressing trick by counting to ten. It didn't help.

"Kez, I know you're really angry, but we've been through this before. Cat is having a rough time and she needs to talk it over," Ollie explained.

"Well, why does she have to talk to *you* about it all the time?" snapped Kerry again, amazing herself at her forcefulness.

"For a start, how can you say that? She was talking to you about it on Sunday, wasn't she?"

Kerry was stumped for a second. "Yeah, but she didn't go throwing her arms around me and slobbering on me!"

"D'you realise how silly that sounds?" said Ollie, half laughing despite the situation. "Look, I think she knows she can trust me. I mean, if we can survive that stupid time we 'went out' together and still be friends after that, then, well..."

As Ollie's argument fizzled out, Kerry shivered slightly and had the uneasy feeling that maybe, just maybe, she'd over-reacted. Again. But there was something still not right...

"So, what's supposed to be up with her now?" Kerry asked, defrosting ever so slightly.

"It's this guy she's going out with – she told you about that, right?"

Kerry nodded.

"Well, now her mum's apparently banned her from seeing him."

"Uh-huh. So, she still hasn't said who he is?"

"No, and I'm not about to pressure her about it. She's obviously got a good reason for keeping it to herself. But listen, what's up with you, Kerry?" he asked, puzzled by her relatively uncaring response. "You don't seem that bothered about what Cat's going through."

"It's– it's not that," Kerry answered, suddenly feeling flustered and full of doubts. She was crazy about Ollie and he seemed to be totally on Cat's side, unlike Sonja, and even Maya.

Who was right? Whose opinion could she trust?

"Well, what is it?" he asked her, desperate to know what was going on in her mind.

"It's just that, uh, Maya thinks Cat's making up the boyfriend thing just for attention," said Kerry, biting her lip nervously.

"What?" gasped Ollie.

"And Sonja thinks she's trying to break us up."

"Sonja thinks *what*? Where did she get *that* from?"

"Just things like Cat making out that Elaine wanted you to join her... and, you know, all that misunderstanding on Sunday."

"But that's all it was! God, I can't believe Sonja came out with that... Splitting me and you up? What a joke!" Ollie looked at Kerry with incredulity. "And Maya! I thought she was the brainy one of us all!"

Now that he put it that way, it *did* all sound kind of ridiculous. But there was *still* something bothering Kerry...

"Ollie?"

"Yeah?"

"That kiss. It just seemed so– so intense..."

Ollie unsettled Kerry by starting to laugh. He leant across the table and grabbed her hand, tilting his head towards her and placing her fingers just above his ear.

"Find any gaps?" he grinned at her.

"What do you mean?" She found herself involuntarily smiling back at him.

"Any bald spots? Where she grabbed me by the hair?"

"Huh?"

"Well, *you* try saying no to Catrina Osgood when she's pulling you towards her by the scalp and suctioning the words out of your mouth!"

They both stopped smiling for a second and paused, staring fondly into each other's eyes – silently knowing how close they'd come to falling out and falling for each other all over again.

Ollie gently rubbed his head against the hand that was cupped by his ear.

"Are you two going to kiss now?"

Lewis stood in the doorway, looking faintly sick.

CHAPTER 17

• •

OLLIE AND KERRY RALLY ROUND

"Look, I'm under no illusions about Catrina," said Ollie, as Kerry helped Lewis on with his jacket while her little brother hummed some silly song under his breath. "She brings a lot of trouble on her own head, I know."

Kerry laughed ruefully and nodded.

"But I think it's really out of order for Sonja and Maya to come out with that stuff about her and, as her mates, I think me and you should, y'know, rally round her. What do you reckon?"

"Sure – you're right," Kerry agreed, hoping that Lewis wasn't going to hum any louder. "We are all meant to be friends, aren't we?"

"Too right. Look, what about the two of us arranging to meet her and helping her talk things through? I could give her a call and fix something up."

"Fine, just let me know where and when. Shush, Lew!"

Lewis looked up at his sister mischievously and carried on mouthing his funny little song.

"Hey, Lewis, you'd better go downstairs and wait by the front door for your sister, 'cause this bit might make you feel ill again," Ollie joked, pulling Kerry close.

As he kissed her, Kerry hoped he couldn't make out what Lewis was singing as he skipped down the stairs.

"*Catrina's a clown! Catrina's a clown! Catrina's a...*"

● ● ●

Cat fumbled with a beer mat and looked forlorn.

Kerry, who was normally the first with kind words, struggled to find something to say. Not because she didn't feel for Cat – she did – but because she felt so guilty at having misjudged her.

"Ollie's been brilliant, he really has," sniffed Cat, gazing over at the bar where he was getting them all a drink (orange juice spritzers all round – Ollie's mum wasn't about to lose her licence over her son and his friends).

"I'm glad," said Kerry warmly, proud of having a boyfriend who was so kind and understanding.

"All the hours and hours he's put in, just listening to my moans," Cat continued mournfully.

Hours and hours? thought Kerry fleetingly.

"Just letting me open up to him to get it all off my chest. Letting me cry on his shoulder..."

For some reason, Kerry found the allusions to body parts slightly discomfiting.

"I feel *so* close to him – you know what I mean?" she said, suddenly spinning her gaze away from Ollie and looking directly and meaningfully into Kerry's eyes.

"Mmmm," muttered Kerry non-committally. She didn't know what Cat's meaningful look was meant to convey, but she knew it made her uncomfortable.

"OK, girls?" said Ollie, sloshing the glasses down on the table messily.

"No wonder your folks haven't encouraged you to work here," said Cat sarkily, pulling a couple of serviettes out of the dispenser and mopping up the spills.

"Well, I'm under age for any of the fun jobs round here, so I'm better off working for Nick anyway – until I get my multi-million pound record deal, of course," Ollie grinned.

A black look crossed Cat's face and Ollie quickly remembered the point of this get-together – to talk about Cat's traumas.

"So, how are things with your mum?" he asked gently.

"Bad," shrugged Cat. "She's... she's refusing point blank to even talk to me now."

"What, about not seeing... this boy?" Kerry chipped in.

"No – I mean *totally* not talking to me."

Kerry forgot her recent niggles of irritation and was overwhelmed with pity for Cat. How awful it must be for your mum to behave that way towards you. Even though Kerry was sometimes irked by her own mum and her tendency to pay more attention to Lewis, she knew that her mother would never alienate her own daughter like that.

"Since when? Since she said you couldn't see... this guy?" asked Ollie, struggling to get the conversation going around such intangible elements as a main character who was shrouded in secrecy.

"Uh-huh," Cat answered, her long-lashed eyes dropping downwards.

"And so she still won't explain why she wants you to stop seeing this person?" Ollie pushed on with his questioning.

"It's obvious, isn't it? She's jealous. She can't stand to see me happy!"

Kerry was lost between sympathy and, well, being lost. Everything Cat had said on the subject, either to her or Ollie, seemed so vague.

Why was Cat's mum suddenly so jealous of her? Who was this mystery boy she was seeing? When was Cat seeing him and why was he still a mystery? Kerry looked from Ollie's concerned face to Cat's troubled one and struggled to understand quite what was going on.

"God, I can't believe she's being such a bitch to you!" said Ollie heatedly. "Trying to interfere in your life like that!"

Cat gave him a wan, sad smile.

"But how can she stop you from doing whatever you want? With her work, she's never home anyway, that's what you always say..." Kerry piped up. "And you're sixteen, so it's not like she can exactly lock you in your room, is it?"

It was meant to be a helpful statement, but the dead-eyed stare that Cat was giving her didn't seem to indicate that she was appreciative of Kerry's words.

"Well, I think—"

But before he could continue, Ollie was drowned out by a clattering of heavy feet and ear-splitting, bellowing laughter as Ollie's dad, Stuart, and Nick came down into the bar from the upstairs flat.

They may have been brothers but, apart from their beer bellies, the only thing that Stuart (all sharp-dressing casual and shorn, grey hair) and Nick (Cuban heels, rock T-shirt and ponytail) had in common was boasting about how well their businesses were doing and arguing about music that was at least twenty years out of date.

"Well, I'll be interested to see how you wangle *that* past your accountant..." Ollie's dad chuckled wryly.

"Yeah? You wait and see, mate... Oh hi, Ol!" Nick said cheerfully, spotting his nephew. Then, seeing the girls, his smile seemed to fade. "Right, better be going..."

Nick bounded towards the door before anyone could reply, giving Ollie's mum a quick "Catch you later, Sharon!" over his shoulder.

"As I was saying," said Ollie, turning back to the matter in hand and giving Kerry's hand a loving squeeze, "Cat, I really think that you might feel better if you told me and Kerry who it is that you've been seeing. I mean, you don't *have* to, but it might be a weight off your mind..."

"Sure. Why not," said Cat, with what looked suspiciously like a sneer. "It's Nick. I'm seeing Nick."

CHAPTER 18

● ●

SONJA TAKES CHARGE

"Could I speak to Sylvia Osgood, please?"

Kerry sat on the stairs and hugged her knees tightly to her chest. The cringe factor of this call was making her curl up with awkwardness, but at least it was Sonja sitting on the chair with the phone pressed against her ear and not Kerry. Mind you, Kerry wouldn't even have had the courage to *make* the call in the first place. Thank God for Sonja and her fearlessness!

"*Sorry?* Oh, no, Kerry – *I'm* sorry! I shouldn't have gone all huffy on you like a big kid," Sonja had said when Kerry caught up with her at college earlier and apologised.

It was a relief to Kerry that she'd been able to make up so easily with Sonja. The strain of dealing with any awkwardness between them was too much on top of all the drama and intrigue going on.

"*Nick? You've* got to be *kidding* me! Sleazy Nick?!" Sonja had gasped, when Kerry had guiltily spilled out Cat's confession of the previous evening. It wasn't just sheer gossip value that had made Kerry tell. She had promised Ollie that she'd try to help Cat somehow and she was completely stumped as to what to do.

The only person she could turn to for inspiration was Sonja. And while Sonja might not be a hundred per cent there for Cat, at least she knew Cat's background and family history better than anyone.

"No wonder Auntie Sylvia's going ballistic! The thought of Cat going out with Nick – yuck! He's so old and creepy!" Sonja had said unhelpfully when they got back to her house and could talk in private.

"You've said plenty of times that Nick's a laugh," said Kerry defensively, although she didn't really understand why she was taking that tack. The thought of Nick and Cat together had freaked her out so much she hadn't been able to sleep properly the night before. Just imagining them together...

"Well, it's one thing to think someone's a laugh, but when a guy who must be nudging forty – with *very* dodgy taste in clothes and hairstyles – goes out with someone who's sixteen, it's most definitely creepy," Sonja retorted, pulling a face and shuddering. "So how long's this been going on for?"

"She didn't say. Like I told you, she just blurted out that she was seeing Nick then did a runner."

"And you think she's pulled a sickie today?"

"Well, I asked around and she's not been in any of her classes."

"Do you think she's skiving because she doesn't want to face you after her little announcement? I sure would be embarrassed if I was her."

"I don't know," shrugged Kerry. Her mind was working overtime with worry. Was it something as simple as being embarrassed about what she'd divulged or was she half-way up the motorway to Gretna Green with Nick, as they spoke?

"Hey, you do realise something?" Sonja butted into her thoughts. "Cat must be the secret girlfriend that Nick's been keeping under wraps all this time!"

"Yeah, Ollie said that last night…"

"What's Ollie making of all this?"

"Oh, he's completely freaked out! He's got it into his head that Nick's taking advantage of Cat. He's going to confront him about it when Nick comes in to the End for the takings."

"Ooh, I'd love to be a fly on the wall for that one!"

"Sonja!" Kerry reproved her friend. "The point is, Ollie's really worried about Cat. So what do you think we should do to help her? Do you think we maybe ought to go round and see her?"

Sonja sobered up and looked thoughtful for a second. She still couldn't bring herself to quite trust Cat's motives in all this. God knows that girl had schemed and plotted plenty of times in the past! But Sonja had to admit to a reluctant soft spot for her irritating relation.

Growing up in a pretty cool family, with pretty relaxed parents and plenty of everything, Sonja had always felt sorry for her attention-seeking younger cousin, who had to live with someone as prickly as her mum Sylvia and as difficult as her dad (before he upped and left). This was the reason Sonja had always let Cat tag along – out of pure sympathy for the stroppy minx, rather than for her often less-than-loveable character.

And now, if Cat *was* seeing someone as ridiculously unsuitable as Nick, it didn't come as a great surprise to Sonja. Neither of Cat's parents had exactly been great role models of love for her to copy...

"No – let's see what my darling aunt's got to say first," said Sonja, walking out into the hall and flicking through her parents' phone book for Sylvia's work number. "She might find it easy to bully Cat, but *I'm* not frightened of her."

And so here they were – two friends about to help put right the suffering of another friend. Except Kerry couldn't stand the tension any more and, as soon as she heard Sonja say, "Auntie Sylvia? Is that you?", she fled upstairs and locked herself in the loo.

After sloshing water noisily around the basin for a few minutes and pointlessly flushing the loo a couple of times, Kerry felt brave enough to open the bathroom door and gauge how the conversation was going. But instead of words – heated or otherwise – she was relieved to hear the dull *ping*! of the receiver dropping back into place.

"Well? How did it go?" she asked tentatively, tiptoeing down the thickly carpeted stairs and bending to peek at Sonja through the banisters.

Sonja sat on the chair by the phone table with an expression on her face that was hard to read.

"Well?" Kerry repeated.

"*That* was interesting," Sonja said at last.

"Uh-huh? How?" Kerry asked, taking up her previous position on the bottom steps.

"It was a *slightly* different interpretation of events than Catrina's..."

"In what way?"

"In that Sylvia says that *Catrina's* the one who's being the unreasonable bitch at home. And she's also the one who's refusing to talk."

"But why would she be like that?" asked Kerry, aghast. "Do you believe your aunt more than Cat?"

"Well, I think I do, considering what else she had to say."

"Which was?"

"Which was that she *hasn't* banned Cat from seeing Nick – or any other boyfriend for that matter – mainly because Cat doesn't have one."

"One what?" asked Kerry, by now completely thrown.

"*Boyfriend*, stupid."

"What?"

"No, wait, it gets better," said Sonja, her voice dripping with irony. "It turns out that the only person with a new boyfriend in their house is *Sylvia*, and the one who's flipping out with jealousy – is *Cat*."

CHAPTER 19

● ●

THE TRUTH, THE WHOLE TRUTH AND NOTHING LIKE THE TRUTH

"So Mrs Osgood wasn't too chuffed, then?"

"No," said Sonja breathlessly, struggling to keep up with Kerry's hurried pace. "I think the way she hung up on me at the end says it all, really."

Kerry grimaced – it was too awful! Any minute now, Ollie was about to lash out at Nick, who was more or less a mate as well as an uncle, and accuse him of having his wicked way with poor, defenceless Cat.

That was a joke! Cat was about as defenceless as a viper...

Kerry glanced at her watch. They *might* still manage to get round to the End before Nick ambled in. Hopefully, he had headed off for a pint with Bryan after closing up the record shop. That would give Sonja and Kerry plenty of time to let Ollie know the latest developments before things really blew up.

And Nick *would* have been off sampling the delights of a drink or three in the Railway Tavern if he hadn't got a date that night. Bryan, sitting alone at a sticky table by the window with his evening meal of a pint of Guinness and a cheese toastie, glanced up from his *NME* and absently watched Kerry and Sonja scurry into the End-of-the-Line café.

Not that he knew which one was Kerry and which one was Sonja. In fact, one of them might be the one with that hippy name, Maya. He never managed to remember which girl was which in Ollie's troupe of mates. Except for that Catrina ... oh, yes, he knew which one *she* was. Bryan shuddered slightly and turned his attention back to the *NME*.

Tripping up the single step into the café, Kerry and Sonja shoved the tinkling door open in unison and knew immediately that they were too late.

"Stop denying it!" they heard Ollie yell.

"Are you crazy!" Nick roared back. "What the hell has she told you?"

Anna was serving a trayful of burgers and

milkshakes to a loud crowd of thirteen-year-olds. Out of the corner of her eye, Kerry noticed that one of the squawking horde was Maya's little sister, Sunny. Out on a school night? How had she managed that one? Kerry wondered, knowing how strict Maya's parents were.

But all that flashed through her mind in a split second. What occupied her more was the sound of shouting coming from the kitchen. Anna looked up at the two girls with concern in her eyes.

"Go through," she mouthed, nodding in the direction of the yelling.

The girls flashed by her, past the counter and along the corridor to the Staff Only door.

"That little bitch! What's she playing at?" bellowed Nick.

"Don't you call her a bitch!" retaliated Ollie.

Steam belching from a pot on the range behind Nick looked to Sonja and Kerry as if it was coming out of his ears. His face was pink and pinched enough with anger for that to be possible, but then Ollie's was much the same. In fact Ollie and Nick appeared to be about half a kitchen and two more insults away from landing a punch on each other.

Kerry felt a shiver of alarm to see her normally gentle boy acting so aggressively.

"Yeah? Well, I can think of better words to use, but not in front of the ladies here," Nick retorted, pointing to Sonja and Kerry. They'd never seen him this irate before. Laid-back was the only gear that Nick usually operated in.

"Yeah? Hey, you're a real tough guy, aren't you?" Ollie snarled.

"That's it! I'm going to get this sorted," said Nick darkly, pushing up the sleeves of his leather jacket and storming out of the back door.

"What does he mean?" Kerry's voice wobbled.

Ollie seemed oblivious to her words and spat a curse at the still-shuddering door.

"Ol, it's not his fault," Sonja broke in to his black mood. "Nick's not seeing Cat – she made it all up."

"Are you crazy?" said Ollie, staring at her with disbelief. "Are you *still* coming out with that stuff?"

"No, it's true – Sonja found out from Cat's mum!" Kerry backed her friend up quickly.

"*Kerry!*" gasped Ollie, with a look of dismay and betrayal crossing his face.

"Honestly, Ollie, it's true!" Kerry crumpled under his distrusting gaze.

"I'm telling you – she made it up!" Sonja persisted. "Nick isn't guilty of... of mucking around with Cat!"

"Of course, he's guilty!" Ollie said with exasperation. "Otherwise, why would he be so worked up?"

"I can tell you why," said Anna, joining the others in the kitchen.

"What do you mean?" asked Ollie, as Sonja and Kerry looked on in surprise. What did Anna have to do with any of this?

"Hey, waitress, what about a bit of service?" yelled a thirteen-year-old voice from the café beyond, accompanied by much finger-clicking and giggling.

"Shut it!" Anna yelled uncharacteristically through the serving hatch. Chastened, the yeller did indeed shut it.

"Now, you lot, go and get yourself a table. You too," she said to Ollie, flapping him away with her apron. "I'll be out in a second."

Like the thirteen-year-olds, Ollie, Sonja and Kerry did as they were told.

• • •

The Verve's *Bittersweet Symphony* blasted out of the ancient jukebox. It was one of the few 'new' records that Nick allowed in his precious '50s find.

Most of the vinyl in there was Nick's decades-old

choice – all reminders of his favourite bands and his days on the road.

Anna pressed another couple of buttons – the music would give them some privacy to talk without being overheard – and walked over to join the others.

"Hey, Miss, have you got any ketch—"

In one smooth movement, Anna grabbed a bottle of tomato sauce off the counter and plonked it on the table in front of one of Sunny's mates without breaking her stride.

Ollie was sitting at the booth by the window with his face hidden in his hands. Kerry and Sonja sat on the other side of the table, gazing sympathetically at the top of his head.

"Budge up," said Anna, forcing Ollie out of his pained reverie. He budged up, leaving her plenty of room to sit down. "Sorry, I just had to get the last of that order out of the way."

"So, Anna... I've just fallen out with someone who's not only my relative but my boss, and all in defence of someone who I thought was my friend," said Ollie, managing a tired smile and looking more like his old self. "Got any light to shed on this mess?"

"A bit," shrugged Anna, "but I didn't know the stuff about Catrina saying she was going out with Nick. *That* was news."

The other three looked at Anna quizzically. Apart from Ollie – who exchanged banter with her in the café when their shifts coincided – none of the others had had much of a conversation with her. And yet here she was, apparently about to unravel some of the tangle they'd found themselves in.

"Well, I figured out all that from the screaming in the kitchen," Anna explained, assuming their expressions were to do with how she'd cottoned on to Nick and Cat's supposed relationship.

Ollie winced and nodded, realising for the first time the volume of his slanging match with his uncle.

"So what *do* you know?" asked Sonja, taking the initiative.

Anna leant her crossed arms on the table and looked in particular at Ollie.

"I know why Nick was so defensive and angry."

"Why?" said Ollie, mortified at how badly he'd goofed where his uncle was concerned.

"The girlfriend he's kept hidden away. I know who it is."

Anna felt three sets of eyes burning into her and spilled her secret...

CHAPTER 20

●●●●●●●●●●●●●●●●●●●●●●●●●●

THE ALL-SEEING ANNA

"*Sylvia*?!" croaked Sonja.

"Sonja's *aunt*?!" gasped Kerry, staring first at Sonja's shocked face then back at Anna.

"Cat's *mum*?!" Ollie gulped.

"One and the same," Anna nodded sagely. "Not that I know her. I only saw her once waiting in the car when Nick nipped in for his mobile phone."

Nobody felt capable of saying anything, so Anna carried on with her explanation.

"I was up in the flat – I could see her out the window. She looked very... sophisticated. Not his type at all."

They all thought of the fluffy-haired rock chicks that Nick usually had on his arm. Then visualised Cat's very together, terribly immaculate mother – who looked permanently ironed, from the tips of her super-smooth bob to the power suits she lived in. It didn't add up. No wonder Nick hadn't revealed – or been allowed to reveal – this particular dalliance.

"Nick spoke to me about it the next day and swore me to secrecy," Anna continued. "He said Cat's mum was a real bit of class and he didn't want to mess it up with her. And she didn't want you—" she motioned towards Ollie "—or any of Cat's friends knowing."

"Probably because she'd be really embarrassed at anyone finding out she's dating the only man in Winstead who still thinks cowboy boots and thrash metal are in," quipped Ollie, in spite of himself.

"But how on earth did they meet?" Sonja wondered out loud. "I can't see my aunt hanging out down at the Railway Tavern or any of the other dives Nick usually goes to."

"He told me that too. It was at that gym he's been going to – the one up at the tennis club," Anna explained.

"So that's why he's kept up this exercise kick for so long!" said Ollie, as things became clearer. "There had to be a big incentive for him to keep going to the gym or he'd have been back to his old beer-belly swelling ways by now."

"But what does Cat's mum see in him?" asked Kerry.

"A bit of rough?" guessed Ollie.

"I think 'opposites attract' is the more PC way to say it," smiled Anna.

"Wait a minute – do you think Cat knew about her mum and Nick?" Sonja said suddenly.

"Oh, yes – she did," nodded Anna. "Nick said Cat's mum had specifically told her not to go gossiping about her private life to all of you lot."

"What a nerve! What does Sylvia think we're like?" gasped Sonja. "As if we'd be interested in her stupid love-life..."

"Of *course* we would! What are we doing now?!" Ollie laughed. "I reckon Cat's mum had the right idea!"

"Whatever," Anna smiled. "I just felt sorry for Nick. He obviously thought I'd spotted Cat's mum and felt he had to take me into his confidence. I didn't have the heart to say that I wouldn't have known who she was if he hadn't told me."

"Nick and Cat's mum..." mused Kerry dazedly, then shook herself as a thought struck her. "But why did Cat make out that *she* was the one going out with Nick?"

"To get attention?" suggested Anna. She didn't know the ins and outs of this particular situation, but she'd observed everyone in the crowd for long enough to get a good handle on each of them.

And Cat seemed to be a typical 'Me! Me! Me!' scene-stealer from where Anna stood.

"But what's the point in telling us – her mates – such a big lie just for attention?" asked Kerry. "We were bound to find out about it!"

"I don't think people who tell lies like this really think much about the consequences when they do it. As long as they're getting a reaction, that's what counts," Anna shrugged. "It's just Cat's way of boosting her low self-esteem."

"Low self-esteem? She's the biggest show-off in the world!" Sonja couldn't help saying, although she knew, deep down, that there was truth in what Anna was saying.

"It's pretty common for people with the lowest self-esteem to cover it up with big talk and bluster." Anna felt confident of her diagnosis of Cat's behaviour. In an effort to sort out her own life, she'd read a lot about stuff like this. She could never resist buying self-help psychology books with her not-too-spectacular wages, and they weighed down the bookshelves in her bedsit upstairs.

"But I still don't get it," Ollie shook his head.

"Yeah, but think about it," said Sonja, to whom everything was now starting to make sense. "Cat's always been a flirt – and it's not an excuse or anything – but it could be because her dad left her when she was young. It's like she craves attention from men."

"So? What's that got to do with her mum and Nick?" Ollie asked, struggling to understand.

"Well, Cat and her mum have always been pretty competitive with each other, so she was always going to be jealous of someone finding her mum attractive and not her."

"'Specially since she's found out that her mum's boyfriend is Nick," Kerry added. "I mean, he's like part of Cat's world, isn't he, with all of us hanging out here in the caff? It's like her mum's stolen something that belonged to *her*."

"Yeah, but while we're sitting here feeling sorry for her all of a sudden, don't forget what else Cat's been up to lately," Sonja threw in, glancing from Ollie to Kerry. "Like trying to break you two up."

"Aw, Sonja, I still don't think—"

"Ollie, you've got to trust me on this one," Sonja insisted. "I've been keeping an eye on her. Ever since she realised that something might be going on with you two, she's been all over you like a rash and made herself pretty busy filling Kerry's head full of doubts."

"Look, I don't know what's been going on between all of you, but I do think you ought to try and help her out, if she's a friend," Anna butted in. "I mean, I don't think she's done all this to be bitchy. It sounds more like she's just really messed up emotionally."

"You're right," said Ollie, wondering how Anna could work out more about the situation in one brief conversation than any of them had in all this time.

"And if I were you," said Anna to all three of them, "I'd go straight round to her place 'cause I reckon she'll be getting an earful from Nick right now."

Ollie, Sonja and Kerry stared at each other in alarm.

"But it'll take us at least half an hour to get round to Cat's, even if we hurry!" Kerry pointed out.

"Ollie, what's Matt doing tonight?"

Ollie stared at Sonja and couldn't quite figure out for a second what that had to do with anything.

"Nothing, as far as I know."

"Well, he lives closest to Cat and he's got a car," Sonja reasoned. "If we phone him, he could be there in a couple of minutes."

"What — Matt going to Catrina's rescue? To defend her honour? That's a laugh!" Ollie pointed out.

"All that stuff is in the past, Ol!"

"She's not going to see it that way, though,

Sonny. Matt, of all people, witnessing what a mess she's made of things – it would be like a slap in the face!"

"Some old failed romance with Matt is hardly going to be the main thing in her mind right now!" Sonja retorted.

"Well, I think—"

But while Ollie and Sonja were trying to analyse the strange inner workings of Cat's mind and figure out what to do, Kerry was already dialling Matt's number on the café's payphone.

• • •

"Mmm, this should be interesting," said Sonja pointing out three cars parked in the street outside the modern mansion block where Cat lived.

Her Auntie Sylvia's silver Vectra was closest to them, in a residents' only space, while Matt's dark blue Golf was further along, overshadowed by Nick's chunky Shogun jeep.

"Looks like we're fashionably late for the party," joked Ollie, but he wasn't smiling.

Climbing the stairs to the third-floor flat, they could all hear the muffled sound of raised voices.

"You stupid, stupid girl!"

"But, Mum! I didn't– I didn't mean to—"

"I can't be bothered with this childish

behaviour, Catrina. I really can't!"

"But, Mum! Honest! Please..."

Sonja stared at Kerry and Ollie who, like her, were frozen outside the front door. Quickly, she pressed the doorbell.

"Oh good God! What are you lot? The cavalry?" sighed Cat's mum, opening the door to her niece and her two friends.

She turned away from them and walked back towards the kitchen. They took the fact that she hadn't slammed the door on them to be the closest thing to an invitation they were likely to get.

"Nick, come on – let's go. I've had enough of this farce," barked Cat's mum, scooping up her packet of cigarettes and gold lighter from the kitchen table and running her other hand through her shiny helmet of hair.

Still in the short hallway behind her, Sonja, Ollie and Kerry all pressed themselves against the expensive wallpaper and made way for Sylvia to stride past them, with a slightly bashful-looking Nick in tow. He nodded imperceptibly towards them and nervously shoved the sleeves of his leather jacket further up his arms.

As the front door latch clicked shut, they all breathed a collective sigh of relief, and only then ventured towards the kitchen.

None of them was quite expecting the sight that met their eyes.

Matt was sitting on the far side of the kitchen table, cradling a silently sobbing Catrina in his arms, gently rocking her to and fro.

• • •

"I just couldn't *stand* to see you two in love."

Kerry and Ollie both felt delicious prickles of embarrassment mixed with revelation race across their skin. Neither had brought up the 'L' word yet; it was strange and exciting to hear someone say it out loud.

Cat crumpled up another soggy tissue and chucked it towards the steadily growing pile on the kitchen table.

"I've never been lucky when it comes to boys," she shrugged sadly, seemingly oblivious to Matt – who was still sitting protectively next to her – and their whole tangled past.

Of course that could be a dig, innocently disguised, thought Kerry, who didn't underestimate Cat's powers of manipulation for one second now. Cat had admitted it all to them in the last hour: the lie about dating Nick; the way she'd deliberately tried to drive a wedge between Kerry and Ollie through misinformation and half-truths.

Now Cat was trying to explain to the others – and to herself – why she'd done it.

"Then I see you two," she sniffed, pointing at Ollie and Kerry, "all cosy together, and I keep thinking – why not me? Why couldn't it have worked out with you and me, Ollie?"

"Well, what about the fact that we didn't fancy each other?" said Ollie, giving her a lopsided grin. He hoped she wasn't going to start on Matt next. That was a whole can of worms that nobody, least of all Matt, wanted opened up again.

"I know, I know," shrugged Cat. "But why doesn't anyone want to go out with me? What's wrong with me?"

With an ear-splitting trumpet, she blew her nose again. Everyone waited in silence for her next proclamation.

"And when even my *mother* ends up with a boyfriend, I just thought – that's it! I'm a failure..."

"But was it the fact that she was seeing Nick that bothered you?" Ollie asked gently.

"No! Well, a bit..." Cat alternately shook then nodded her head. "I mean, *I'm* the young, pretty one – *she's* past it!"

Sonja and Matt exchanged withering glances at Cat's lack of modesty and tact, but let it pass.

"And it just pissed me off that she can end up with someone while I'm on my own. And Nick – well, he's someone I know! I don't go barging into her world; why should she get involved with mine?"

"OK, I guess we all get your point," Ollie pacified her. "But why did you tell us you were going out with Nick?"

"Dunno, really..." said Cat, dabbing at her mascara-streaked cheeks. "I just wanted to pretend to have a boyfriend so I could feel a bit more *special* or important – or something, I guess."

"Yeah, but if you'd carried on with the secret boyfriend story, we wouldn't have been any the wiser," Sonja interrupted. "Why did you go and tell Ollie and Kerry that it was Nick?"

"I don't know – it just came out. I just saw you and you," sighed Cat, looking at Kerry and Ollie, "being all lovey-dovey in the pub together and flipped out. I wanted to shock you. So I came up with the first thing I could think of."

"But *Nick*!" Ollie cackled. "You could have come up with a better pretend boyfriend than him, surely!"

Along with the others, Kerry started laughing. Trust Ollie to try and lighten the atmosphere. She looked over at him lovingly, happy to see his cheeky grin back in place.

"So anyone up for a bet?" Ollie asked, clapping his hands together and glancing round the table.

"What on?" asked Sonja, wondering what Ollie was playing at.

"How long the budding romance is going to last between my dopey uncle and your old witch of a mother," he proclaimed, giving a nod in Cat's direction. Giggles started to overcome her snivelling.

"Cool! I bet a tenner that it doesn't last the night!" said Matt enthusiastically. "You should have seen the look on Nick's face when Cat's mum turned into a shrieking dragon. He looked ready to turn and run right there and then!"

"Oh, you guys are the best!" gushed Cat, standing up and reaching across to plant wet-nosed kisses and hugs on Matt, Sonja and now Kerry.

Wiping the wet patch off her cheek, Sonja turned to Kerry. "Why don't we give Joe and Maya a call and see if they fancy coming round? We might as well try and make this more of a party than a wake."

"Good idea," nodded Ollie.

"Oh yes, let's!" Cat sniffed, looking strangely young now that she had sobbed off all her make-up.

"Sure," said Kerry. "I'll go and give them a call right now."

"Kerry, you're a darling, you really are!" Cat gave her a wobbly smile as Kerry headed out of the room.

It is better to forgive than... something, thought Kerry warmly, trying to dredge her memory for the appropriate phrase.

Yeah, so Cat could be a pain in the neck, but she'd been going through a harder time than any of them had realised.

And it's not as though she's spoiled anything between me and Ollie, Kerry realised. *In fact, if anything, it's made us stronger...*

Smiling at the sounds of laughter and chat coming from the kitchen, Kerry stretched the cord of the phone so that she could peek back along the hall at her friends.

"Hello?" said Joe, hearing only a deep sigh at the other end of the line. "Hello?"

Will Cat never learn? thought Kerry in the darkness of the corridor, as she watched Ollie trying to struggle out of Cat's over-enthusiastic hug and let's-make-up embrace.

Tongues and everything, as Lewis would have said...

Sugar
SECRETS...

...& Freedom

"Sounds like your Sunday night was as bad as mine," sighed Maya.

"Yeah?" said Joe. "What's happened with you?"

Joe was keen to hear someone else's moans – it made him feel better about his own predicament. He'd just told his friends about the previous evening, which had gone downhill after he'd agreed to the parental visit.

His mum had made him call up his father there and then, which was bad enough, but after a few awkward words and arrangements, his dad had had the not-so-brilliant notion to pass him on to Gillian. Trying to make polite conversation with the woman who your dad had run off with wasn't exactly the easiest thing in the world.

A sudden thump on his arm brought Joe down to earth again.

"What are you talking about now? You're not still moaning on about your dad are you, Joe?" said Ollie playfully, pulling a seat from another table and joining his friends at the booth in the big bay window of the café.

He knew how difficult Joe found the whole situation and, while he was glad that his friend was opening up about it in front of the others, but he instinctively felt that a bit of humour would lighten things up.

"And what are you doing, Ollie?" Sonja teased him. "Skiving off on another break?"

"Well, there's hardly anyone in except you lot," he grinned, gazing round the café. "And I'm sure my fellow workers can spare me for a moment."

"Oi!" said Anna from behind the counter, flinging a balled-up tea towel at his head.

Stretching out, Matt caught the unravelling cloth neatly, before it landed smack-bang on Catrina's perfectly made-up face.

"Sorry, Catrina!" Anna apologised. "I was aiming for the lazy little git in the apron, but he ducked."

"Don't worry about it, Anna – I'll kick him for you, if you like," Cat replied brightly. "If that's OK with you, Kerry."

Kerry shrugged. "Oh go ahead. He's a rotten boyfriend anyway."

"Why am I a rotten boyfriend?" Ollie blinked pitifully at Kerry.

"'Cause you got us all excited about the club at The Bell on Friday, and you went and got the date wrong!" she said, trying to sound stern – but spoiling it all by breaking into a grin.

"What?" yelped Sonja and Matt in unison.

"OK, I'm guilty – the club is next month. Oops!" shrugged Ollie.

"You mean I went through a whole heap of

hassle with my parents for nothing last night?"

Everyone turned to look at Maya. For the first time, they noticed that her normally serene expression had vanished. Instead, she seemed tense, and brushed her curtains of shiny dark hair back behind her ears in a more agitated way than usual.

"So, uh, what's the story? What went on last night?" asked Joe, realising that he'd already asked this question, but never received an answer.

"Oh, just the usual rubbish," May snapped unhappily. "Just no, you can't do this; no, you can't do that; no, you can't be trusted. That sort of thing."

The others were silent for a second: the one person they never expected to lose their cool was Maya, and here she was on the verge of... something.

"But where did this come from, Maya?" asked Cat, studying her friend's face. She was aware that she never completely understood Maya – after all, Cat invested most of her time thinking about herself – but to see her friend looking so upset was unsettling. "I mean, we know your folks are hot on you studying all the time and everything, but you get on pretty well with them, don't you?"

"Oh, yes," said Maya, laying on the sarcasm thick. "I get on great with them as long as I get good grades, look after my brother and sister, do what I'm told – and have no life!"

Once again, everyone was silenced.

Maya didn't flip out. Maya didn't have problems. She was the one who sailed sensibly through everything; she was the one who was reasoned, calm and balanced, while Cat, Sonja, Joe, Kerry, Matt or Ollie goofed up, stressed out or said the wrong thing.

Maya was untouchable, unshakeable; she was the rock. But now something had shaken her up, and that shook them all up.

"But I thought you kind of got off on all that studying?" said Sonja lamely.

Maya rolled her eyes. "Just because I'm smart doesn't mean I enjoy everything I do."

Coming from anyone else, it might have sounded big-headed, but they all understood what Maya meant. The top stream in every subject was her natural home, and no one could deny how brainy she was.

"OK, so your parents are a bit strict and everything," Sonja continued, trying to make sense of what was going on, "but they don't stop you coming out with us, do they?"

As soon as the words were out of her mouth, everyone realised that that wasn't quite true. There had been plenty of occasions when Maya had bailed out from an outing, and none of them had ever pushed her for an explanation.

Without spelling it out, they understood that when Maya said no, she meant no, and it wasn't necessarily her choice.

"But even during term time, you're here at the End most days after school with us, aren't you?" Kerry ventured, trying to say something positive.

Maya gave a hollow laugh.

"Yes, but only because my parents assume I'm actually at home studying. By the time Mum commutes back from the city and Dad finishes surgery, it's nearly seven. I'm always safely back in my room by then, working hard like the good little daughter I'm supposed to be."

"What about the nights we all go out?" asked Joe, amazed at the notion of Maya being in any way a liar. "What do you tell them, then?"

"Oh, I try to stick to the truth – it's just that I don't tell them the whole truth," she answered, her gaze dropping to the table. "It's like, when I've been to see bands with you guys, well, I tell them that's a concert. And that seems fine, as long as they don't realise it's in the back of a pub or in a venue that has a bar or whatever."

"What about my parties? You come to plenty of them," said Matt.

His house parties were legendary: a den with

its own sound system, a fridge full of pizza and beer – Matt was never short of guests.

"Well, they've never met your dad, but they know who he is," Maya pointed out, referring to Matt's very influential, very rich property developer father. "That makes you sound quite respectable."

Cat burst out laughing. "Mr Love Pants!? Respectable? Who are you kidding?"

Matt shot her a cutting look. The last thing needed at this point was any of Cat's barbed little comments.

"Of course, the other thing is..." Maya hesitated. "Well, they think you're only sixteen."

"What?" Matt burst out, suddenly offended.

"And they think you're still at Bartdale's."

"But I left the place more than a year ago!" he protested, shuddering at the memory of the private school where he'd boarded for more years than he cared to remember.

"Yes, but if I told them you were an 18-year-old unemployed wannabe DJ, who dossed around at his daddy's expense, hosting drunken parties whenever possible, do you think they'd let me set foot in your driveway, never mind your house?"

"Uh, I guess not," said Matt, reeling slightly from Maya's unflattering description of himself.

"Ouch!" said Ollie quietly, wincing as he

watched Matt wither under Maya's gaze.

Matt prided himself on being up with the latest dance music, up with the latest fashion, popular with half the girls in Winstead (make that the county). To find himself reduced to the level of chancer/scrounger on the part of Maya kind of took his breath away.

But then, that was Maya for you. Kerry was just a sweetheart, Sonja was his buddy, and Cat – well, Cat was another matter. But Maya could always slay him with her ultra-direct talking.

"It's just that I've had enough of it," Maya pronounced, closing her eyes and rubbing her forehead with the palm of her hand. A vision of her father reading over her homework before she handed it appeared in her head. Wasn't that what teachers were there for?

"So what are you going to do?" asked Kerry, staring earnestly through her wire specs.

"That's the problem," sighed Maya despairingly, without opening her eyes. "What the hell *can* I do?"

DO YOU YEARN FOR FREEDOM?

Maya's frustrations have suddenly boiled over and are now dominating almost her every thought. But it's a very familiar scenario.

Are your parents driving you crazy? Do you wish you had more say in your own life? Try our quiz and see how you score...

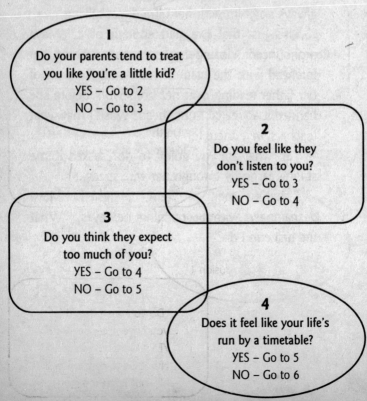

1
Do your parents tend to treat
you like you're a little kid?
YES – Go to 2
NO – Go to 3

2
Do you feel like they
don't listen to you?
YES – Go to 3
NO – Go to 4

3
Do you think they expect
too much of you?
YES – Go to 4
NO – Go to 5

4
Does it feel like your life's
run by a timetable?
YES – Go to 5
NO – Go to 6

5
Are they pressurising
you too much?
YES – Go to 6
NO – Go to 7

6
Do you feel like you're not
allowed to have your own opinions?
YES – Go to 7
NO – Go to 8

7
Are they trying to make you
into a mini version of themselves?
YES – Go to 8
NO – Go to 9

8
Do they often make you feel
like you're letting them down?
YES – Go to 9
NO – Go to 10

9
Do they seem to care about
grades more than you?
YES – Go to 10
NO – Go to conclusion 1

10
Do you wish they'd let
you have more freedom?
YES – Go to conclusion 1
NO – Go to conclusion 2
on the next page

SO, DO YOU YEARN FOR FREEDOM?

• •

Conclusion 1

Your parents drive you mad – but, hey, welcome to the club. What you've got to do is find a way of getting your point of view across, without resorting to screaming arguments: to get them to agree that you'll take on board what they have to say, if they'll do the same for you!

If only Maya could get her parents to see it like that...

Conclusion 2

Most of the time, you have an OK relationship with your parents, but there are times when you resent the way they try to tell you what life's all about. Of course, they're right sometimes – but then so are you!

Maya's relationship with her mum and dad feels unbearable right now – will they ever let her grow up and lead her own life?